PENGUIN BOOKS
A LETTER FROM INDIA

Born in Lahore, Moazzam Sheikh currently makes his home in San Francisco with his wife Amna Ali. He holds degrees in Film and Library Science. He writes fiction in English, Urdu and Punjabi, and translates short fiction from, and into, the three languages mentioned above. His translations of Intizar Husain, *The Circle and Other Stories*, was recently published in Pakistan. He won the Katha Translation award in 1998 for translating from Urdu into English the noted writer Naiyer Mascu's *Sheesha Ghat*. He is currently at work on his own collection of short stories.

A Letter from India

Contemporary Short Stories from Pakistan

EDITED BY
MOAZZAM SHEIKH

PENGUIN BOOKS
An imprint of Penguin Random House

PENGUIN BOOKS

USA | Canada | UK | Ireland | Australia
New Zealand | India | South Africa | China | Singapore

Penguin Books is part of the Penguin Random House group of companies
whose addresses can be found at global.penguinrandomhouse.com

Published by Penguin Random House India Pvt. Ltd
4th Floor, Capital Tower 1, MG Road,
Gurugram 122 002, Haryana, India

First published by Penguin Books India 2004

10 9 8 7 6 5 4 3 2

ISBN 9780143030492

Typeset in Sabon by S. R. Enterprises, New Delhi
Printed at Repro India Limited

www.penguin.co.in

This is a legitimate digitally printed version of the book and therefore might not
have certain extra finishing on the cover.

*This book is dedicated to my mother, Aliya Begum,
to Sultana apa and Zohra apa,
and to Nadir uncle and Razia aunty*

Contents

A harsh Summer night, a lost sea
—Najm Hossain Syed

introduction

The literary history of Pakistani languages, of which there are several, including Punjabi, Sindhi and Pashto, is quite old and rich. All the regional languages have their masterpieces and important works that have held dialogues with the time and place they were created in. These works in the hands of a skillful scholar and translator measure up to the best in the world. The popular Western understanding of classical pre-Pakistani (Indian) literature as being only oral is grossly inadequate. True, most of the old texts were memorized by storytellers and singers, but they were also written down and these works then found their way to the libraries and collections of literate people. Most were written not by wandering dervishes but by writers and intellectuals of the time and one finds in them a sense of history, an awareness of political undercurrents, shifts in literary tastes, negotiation and play with language[s], genre and style, and a lively dialogue with past literary traditions. If there is an unmistakable influence of Persian in Damodar's *Heer* written in the seventeenth century, Waris Shah's *Heer* written a hundred years later shows an amazing sensitivity to the native roots of the Punjabi language and the wide area it was spoken in, a creative response that verges on nationalism. Refreshingly, the reader of classical Punjabi literature also comes across a stunning lack of inhibition towards sexuality and what today's pundits of morality and culture call vulgar language.

Then, all of a sudden, it seems, the literary trail ran into a brick wall.

In South Asia, one of the most harmful legacies of colonialism has been the gradual loss of intimacy with the traditions of one's own soil and culture, history and literature, which are always changing and evolving. The evolution and change reflect a continuum. Colonialism seriously disrupted that continuum. The Urdu writer Intizar Husain loosely refers to the period of colonialism as the era of discontinuity. This fact of gradual loss is truer, and more tragic, with respect to the anglicized class, and of the class that dreams itself as anglicized, which ended up in the driver's seat after the colonialists left.

And thus it is that students in Pakistani schools have ample opportunity to read and understand Shakespeare's plays and poetry as part of their curriculum, whereas a work like *Heer* by Waris Shah reaches people in distorted forms through 'folk wisdom' or movie versions, which are often grossly off the mark. For example, the most quoted and sung verse from Waris Shah's *Heer*, '*doli charh deyaan maariyaan Heer cheekaan* (Heer cried as she mounted the bridal palanquin)' is not from any of the reliably authentic versions of the epic. It was perhaps a late addition made some two hundred years later by a petty scribe or poet. But only a handful of people who happen to be serious readers of classical Punjabi are aware of this.

During my last trip to Lahore I listened in awe to one of my nephews as he discussed Dickens's *David Copperfield* in great detail. I was impressed and a bit disturbed. He is only twelve years old and goes to one of the elite schools of South Asia. When I in turn told him that the countless translations of *The Arabian Nights* had had a tremendous impact on British literature and that Dickens's fiction was a departure from the literature of his time partly due to this influence, he seemed uninterested. It is safe to assume that if I were to engage him on the subject of an important Pakistani writer or a work of classical Punjabi, say, *Puran Bhagat*, he would be at a total loss, a fault not entirely of his own making. I myself was pleasantly surprised to learn recently that the neighbourhood of Icchra in Lahore is actually named after Puran Bhagat's fictional mother.

Only ten years ago I could go on and on about Kafka and not be able to say a word about Naiyer Masud or Bano Qudsiya. This is the situation all over the country. Now consider another case in point. My fifteen-year-old niece, a bright girl and an avid reader of fiction in English who stays clear of pulp unlike most of the English-reading public in Pakistan, could not relate to a well-received anthology of Pakistani short stories in Urdu assigned to her by her teacher at a non-convent, truly modern, Americanized school. After reading a few stories she almost wept, in Urdu, '*Yeh kya hai* (what is this?)!'

Qurratulain Hyder, the winner of the Jnanpith Puraskar in 1991, points out in a preface to another anthology that 'Indian literature of the nineteenth century was largely an extension of Victorian literature.' With the passage of time, our educated classes found it easier to relate to the social and psychological landscape of the Western metropolis than to their own culture. Rather like the protagonist in Amitav Ghosh's wonderful novel *Shadow Lines* who, among other things, is fascinated by the stories about London his cousin Tridib tells him. Indeed, he knows the entire landscape of the house he has never visited before and demonstrates that to May (who loves Tridib) when he visits her. (Of course, Bengal was the first place in India to be fully colonized, militarily and culturally. So the reverse Orientalism of *Shadow Lines* serves as poetic justice.) Yet the reverse swing (unlike in cricket) is achieved in the end at a far higher cost than realized: at the cost of a crippling disconnect. This is a serious problem which affects all aspects of our lives in South Asia, from education to politics, from the status of women to social justice for the disadvantaged. The postcolonial era should have been an era of overcoming the disconnect. Most South Asian governments, however, have neither the intention nor the imagination to fix this problem. It is, then, up to the individual to take up the task.

As I began to question my own relationship with my culture, history and language[s], I realized that sometimes it is pertinent to re-educate oneself in order to reconnect with one's past.

The process of re-acquainting, I must confess, started many years ago as I claimed my dual Pakistani-American identity. It was the subtle racism that permeates every walk of life in the United States that first nudged me to rake up my roots and restore to myself some sense of self-esteem. I did so by going to the local public library to see which South Asian writers' names showed up on the shelves. I found a smattering of names: Ghalib, Tagore, Iqbal, Premchand, Manto. (I would discover later that these were the names that always showed up), and yearned to know more. The first window that opened up to me was *The Colour of Nothingness*, an anthology of Urdu short stories edited by Professor Memon (Penguin). The world it revealed to me was so immense that I felt it would take many lifetimes to explore it. In time, I translated Urdu writers like Naiyer Masud and Intizar Husain and taught myself to read the Devnagari script so I could read Hindi fiction. Training myself to read Punjabi literature in Shahmukhi, a Punjabi script older than its Gurmukhi counterpart but which, surprisingly, has never been taught in schools in West Punjab, was another comic-tragic journey of love and longing. But it was a pleasure to finally be able to read a wealth of modern Punjabi literature from both sides of the border.

When I was asked to edit an anthology of Pakistani short fiction for Penguin India, I wasn't sure at first if I was fit for the job; however, I was painfully aware of the importance of such endeavour and the near absence of anthologies of Pakistani literature. The handful that exist are dominated by a few big names. (I found Asif Farrukhi's *Fire in the Autumn Garden* a refreshing turn in this regard.) Besides, I knew it would give me the opportunity to acquaint myself with Pakistani literature in languages other than English.

The unfortunate fact is that most modern Urdu writers living in the Pakistani side of the Punjab know virtually nothing of their fellow writers in Punjabi. This further gives birth to the attitude that nothing is being written of merit in languages other than English and Urdu. I have always believed that anthologies which highlight literatures in other than state-sanctioned languages go some way towards rooting out ignorance and mistrust and in the process accord humanity to others. This anthology then, among other things, also aims in a small measure to reconnect modern Pakistani literature to its literary past. This is not an attempt to deny the influence from outside (Western or otherwise), but to provide a wider perspective and strike some balance in the reader's mind.

Luckily, I never accepted Rushdie's argument regarding the inferiority of 'vernacular' literature as opposed to its English counterpart. As I started gathering stories for the anthology, I knew I was going to face hurdles he too might have faced had he seriously sought after contemporary Indian literature in languages he is not acquainted with. The hurdles include the difficulty of accessing different literatures, of reaching out to people who have a thorough knowledge of the literature (at least contemporary) in a particular language, then choosing the right stories, and finally connecting with people who could translate from these languages into the target language, which in this case is English. Considering all of the above, *Mirrorwork: Fifty Years of Indian Writing* appears, with all due respect to Rushdie, to be a parody of a serious literary effort. It was more a service to the publishing industry than to the readers.

Not being based in Pakistan, I too found my task to be doubly difficult. But the world of e-mail and internet, among other loyal friends, came to my rescue and saved the day.

I am delighted that at least half of the writers in this book are being anthologized for the first time, and many of them have been translated for the first time. Eleven out of fourteen stories have been translated exclusively for this volume. Talat Abbasi wrote *In His Own Time* for this anthology upon my request, as a sequel to her much acclaimed *Mirage*.

Putting together an anthology presents the inherent problem of having to sometimes leave out writers you admire. Tahira Naqvi, Khalida Husain, Bano Qudsiya, Noorulhuda Shah, Afzal Ahsan Randhawa, Masud Ashar, Anwar Sajjad, Ahsan Wahga and many other writers whose work I would have liked to include, had to be left out in order to give space to newer voices. Also, I found out it was much easier to access stories from those writing in English and residing outside Pakistan. Being a writer in English myself, I have as friends many of these writers, among them Javed Qazi and Tahira Naqvi. But I made a painful decision to include only those who have not been widely read and anthologized. My sincere apologies to Tahira and Javed and others who deserved to be included.

The anthology also reflects a move away from parochialism. If Asad Mohammad Khan's story is an ode to humanity against the backdrop of the Bhopal tragedy, then Sorayya Khan's piece explores a child's dreams that intertwine with her mother's memories of East Pakistan. Fahmida Riaz's intellectual-from-the-East is sexually attracted to a Jewish professor in Berkeley and Azra Waqar's protagonist journeys into the heart of the Bangladesh tragedy.

Above all, I have attempted to include stories that resist being exotic and easy, written for mass consumption, a trend very popular in the United States. Such stories, with the complicity of editors and agents alike, refute the reader's intelligence. Admittedly, I am guilty of making it a little harder for the reader and offer my apology in advance. Roland Barthes has suggested that there are two kinds of writings: readerly and writerly. Readerly writing is for the purpose of pure entertainment, and assumes that the reader is not very intelligent. A writerly text, on the other hand, makes demands and forces the reader to engage with the text to re-construct a (new) meaning of her own. Balzac, too, has said that a serious reader raises herself at par with the writer. This is the journey I have envisioned. I hope readers are willing to undertake the journey with me.

A Letter from India

No book, and this is especially true of anthologies, is brought to fruition single-handedly – rather, it is born of the collective effort of many invisible hands. I've been encouraged in my work, helped and assisted, time and again, by close friends and total strangers alike. One of these strangers did everything in her power to introduce me to the wealth of Punjabi literature, and together we selected and translated stories and got in touch with writers. And now she, Amna Ali, the daughter of the noted Punjabi poet and fiction writer Nadir Ali, is married to me.

My thanks to Asif Farrukhi, Shereen Masud, Raji Pillai (as usual), Pratibha, Ramon, Stewart at the African American Centre at the San Francisco Public Library, Jim and Terry, Ajmal Kamal, Asad Mohammad Khan, Balaji, Ashu Lal and Elizabeth Bell for lending a helping hand, whether it was for getting in touch with a writer, proof-reading, or listening to me read rough drafts time and again. This book is a fruit of their labour as well. Finally, my special thanks to Mridula Mohindra, my editor at Penguin, for painstakingly going over the entire manuscript and really improving the quality of the final product. And I thank you, Karthika, for having faith in a complete stranger. But in the world of literature strange things have been known to happen from time to time. Thanks.

Moazzam Sheikh

the barbarians and the mule

Moazzam Sheikh

'There are no barbarians!'
    '*Each of us seeking to top the other's tale—for*
    that's the rule in this country: Whoever tells *the best story
wins . . .*'

(Jonathan Tel in Spleen; Or, the Goy's Tale)

-1-

*I can feel creatures of all cut crawling around me in the obscurity
of this terrible night (it is one thing to be gazing at the stars at
night, and another to be surrounded by insects, lizards, scorpions,
and snakes), that is: it doesn't surprise me that I have grown to
hate darkness—reluctantly— in most manifestations. Who
wouldn't! That is the question I ask again and again, and the
answer surprises me. Ah (whispered ever so gently), I wouldn't.
I wouldn't only if I weren't afraid—yes, I am afraid, scared to
my shrivelling balls—and it feels I'll never get out of this abyss,
the darkness, the fear of being engulfed by it, of becoming it, the
nocturnal beast in me howls as in grief. But this sudden, or perhaps
not so sudden, shift perplexes me as I used to be quite fascinated
by darkness, partly out of curiosity and partly out of pity; I was
mesmerized by its ability to devour anything, even anger, like a
dark python—even non-existence, like an invisible woman! I
was attracted to the barbarity it offered. But now I am scared,
scared I'll never emerge. It is not that I am afraid of being bitten
to a deeper death by these lowly creatures, nor am I afraid of*

death, for when you flip the coin of life, you learn you have been buying death on an instalment plan—or afraid of turning into a heap of rotting flesh and being discovered weeks later by a crowd's collective pity; no, I am afraid of something else, something more essential than the desire to puff air through my mouth. It is the metamorphosis, certainly, I experience as though once the darkness is over I won't recognize my face, recognize myself . . .

-2-

(The secret of love, the lovers reveal,
   is not to abandon the weak knowingly)
   Waris Shah

He lazily removed his cap and wiped the sweat off his face with it, then smacked it against his right leg, twice, before putting it back on, adjusting the cap's side above his ear. First, he cursed the heat, then kicked the big, cemented boulder to shake the dust from his new army boots or perhaps simply from boredom, he couldn't tell. Soon he began whistling a new catchy song whose words he vaguely remembered, but the tune trailed off, and he fell silent, thinking with a mixture of pride and trepidation, pondering still the reasons that had brought him here from such a long distance. But the distance was a relative concept, he offered. Man's conscience and a sense of duty can even call him to the gardens of death. He looked far ahead into the parched stretch of land, part his and part not, an ambiguous claim, that wretched, ambivalent thing called life, and squinted his eyes at the periphery where he could make out the front line of beaten houses, battered shacks covered with corrugated roofs of grey material. Stretches of barbed wire occasionally glinted in the distance if he moved. The heat had driven everyone inside, even his comrades, except him, so it seemed. Should he pity himself? No, never, he whispered. The occasional glint annoyed him. He looked up, far beyond, to the sky; was it also only part his? What if it is the last sky? No bird in sight. What a ruthless stretch of eternity! He lowered his gaze again.

Moazzam Sheikh

Somewhere in the middle of the barbed wire and him, emerged a nicely paved road, which reminded him of his home country, and bridged over the dirty, unpaved street that crawled to the small town into the distance. The nice road swerved once again and disappeared to the left. Roads and streets fascinated him. He could stare at them for hours, thinking about their metaphorical quality, their resemblance to life, how they lured you to a journey, and how they took you, often, nowhere.

'Some coffee? Do you want some coffee?' came the sergeant's voice from inside the two-room post, behind which at a distance ran a big, long wall running in both directions protecting inhabitants from the barbarians around it. He was a wall too, made of brick and mortar, to protect innocents from the barbarians, the butchers. Behind the wall he could see the upper flats, still unfinished and uninhabited. But these were sacred empty rooms, dearer to him than his own precious life.

'No, thanks, I'm fine,' he answered.

'Oh, I love your accent.' The laughter of other soldiers sitting inside the room resounded and died.

Irritated, yet amused, he looked at the sad and pathetic mule tied to a pole at the side of the rooms. He was conscious of the possibility, rather certain at times of it being a fact, that they were jealous of his toughness precisely because they could detect, see through it a more refined, and poetic soul. He wasn't a thug, like them. He was a soldier poet, not a philosopher king exactly but one who could see beauty in a bullet. The presence of the flee-ridden animal perplexed him, but he was in no mood for asking questions, not on his first day. He would allow himself no distraction. This did not fail to remind him, however, of a story he had read in a literary magazine many years ago. He tried to remember the title of the story, but it eluded him. A Hasid is throwing stones at the exterior of a dance hall and crying aloud *Sabbath! Sabbath!* From one corner of the square emerges a second-hand dealer swatting his donkey with an olive branch while crying *Alte zakhen!* The Hasid first asks the dealer in Yiddish, then in Hebrew if he were a Jew: *Atah yehudi?* The man doesn't answer, perhaps, for fear of being stoned, if he were a Jew indeed. The owner of the mule simply responds by repeating *Alte zakhen!* The poor thing!

Suddenly, then, the face of Layla, his Persian ex-girlfriend, a Sephardic Jew, rose in his mind, shimmering in the heat; uncomfortably he remembered her parting words, 'Your ears are as big as a donkey's; if only you'd ever use 'em,' before she stormed out of the café—and his life. Something made him nostalgic, made him miss the city he'd left behind, the city of writers, both failed and successful. *I could've been a writer, a novelist, a good novelist, if I'd stuck to it.* He was always at unease about his big ears, though the rest of his face contained a certain amount of charm and attraction which women found pleasing. Her last words coloured with the hurt she'd felt at his hands had wounded him deeply, but now, with the distance of time the echo of those parting shots, in fact, amused him. His lips curled in a suppressed smile. Yet, to his amazement, he still could feel the ache, and the smile gave way to that unique feeling of loss.

He took out a packet of cigarettes from inside his trouser pocket. With the cigarette dangling from the side of his lips, he lit the match while keeping an eye on the dirt road and put the packet back. Just then a light wind blew and put out the match before he could light his cigarette. He struck another match, cupping the flame this time, and turned his head towards the post. Just then he tensed up, his hands freezing around the struggling flame. Far into the distance a human head glistened, approaching. He put out the match and tossed the cigarette on to the dirt. His eyes narrowed in fear and uncertainty.

'Saul,' a quiver in his voice.

'What? What's up?' came the reply.

'A mule is on its way here.' With those words out of his mouth, he became aware of the other animal's presence.

All the four soldiers emerged at the slightest notice and looked in the direction of the moving head. But soon there was a sigh of

Moazzam Sheikh

relief as the head acquired a torso accompanied by the head of a small child perched in front on the bar of the bicycle. The heat created a mirage of water between the approaching bicycle and the awaiting men, who realized that it was his first encounter as a reservist on duty. The four smiled, partly from irritation and partly from satisfaction at finding their young recruit alert and doing his duty well. Saul motioned the two soldiers and they reluctantly walked back into the shade.

'You know what to do,' said Saul. 'I'll just watch you from a distance. Don't be intimidated, all right?'

He nodded.

'You can handle the mule,' said the sergeant as he took a few steps back and sipped from his coffee mug.

'But deal with him as you would a snake.' That was Ben, the shortest of all.

The bicycle came to a halt some ten yards from them as he drew his palm up, ordering the man to stop. He had expected the two to be nervous, even scared. The faces of the barbarians were expressionless. But, then, the older man's face, hardened by the sun, broke into a submissive smile. The little boy jumped off the bicycle.

'Move closer,' the young soldier ordered. He felt something essential stiffening in him.

The man started walking with his transport and the boy.

He studied his buddies from the corner of his eye and suddenly he had the feeling of being in a war movie, possibly *The Eagle Has Landed*, and the clouds of uncertainty and heroism hovered just above his head. For some inexplicable reason their vigilance annoyed him, as though the purpose of their presence was not to lend him moral support but to mock him into something he was not willing to do. He resented the tyranny of their silent gaze, their inherent authority; he felt molested. But he knew what to do and was determined to rise to the occasion.

'Where are you coming from?'

'From the village,' answered the man, pointing backwards.

'Does the village have any name?' This time his voice softened unexpectedly. Perhaps, he was aware of his accent.

The man offered the name: 'Dier Yassin.'

The soldier nodded disinterestedly.

'Where are you going?'

'To my house, over there,' the man pointed to the area in the distance where he had been looking earlier.

Slowly but firmly, he took a step closer. 'What's in the sack that's on the back of your bicycle?' His voice regained the confidence that had ebbed a moment ago.

'Food items, habibi.'

'Who is this boy?' (*Did I say that right?*)

'My son.'

'Papers?' (*I'm sure I said it right!*)

The man had already reached for his shirt pocket, and produced the identification papers for him.

'Where is his identification?' he pointed to the boy.

'His name is written on my paper.'

'But where is his paper?'

'He is not an adult.'

'Don't give me that crap and shut up. I can see.'

The man fell silent. The young reservist stared into the man's eyes for a long minute, as though searching for a sign of defiance, but found none; the man's servility, strangely enough, only added to the disgust he'd already felt for these creeps, the enemies of his chosen people. Then he looked at the boy, into his stony eyes; something made him uncomfortable and he looked away.

'Open your duffel,' he said, softening his voice.

The man complied by placing the cloth sack on to the dirt and untied it from the top. The sack revealed mostly food items: rice, lentils, fuava beans.

He ordered them to step back, almost shouting, and he instantly realized he had overreacted. The man obeyed, but the boy stood there beside the items. The father reached for his son's arm and pulled him back.

'Is he deaf?'

'He is a child, habibi.' The man tried to smile.

'Snake is a snake,' he whispered, but loud enough for the rest to hear.

The man's smile disappeared.

He folded the paper.

'Do you not agree?'

The man remained silent, a bit puzzled, perhaps even wounded.

'A snake is a snake whether young or old. Repeat it!' he ordered as he once again challenged the man by looking straight into his eyes. The man's gaze changed from bafflement to cold anger, the young reservist seemed to detect. This only made him happier.

'Repeat if you want to get home today.'

'A snake is . . . a snake . . .' the man paused.

'Whether young or old.'

'Whether . . . young or old.'

'Now you are listening, mule,' but he suppressed the 'mule' part from being overheard clearly, and this bothered him. So he repeated:

'Mule!' aloud.

It was at this point he felt a wave of unexpected enchantment swarming in his heart at finding the man acknowledging his humiliation, his accepted inferiority. But for some acutely bizarre reason Layla's whisper distracted him, *or was it just a laugh?* He became conscious of his ears, and could feel them turning red. But the father and the son were not looking at him. *Thank God!* He was briefly tempted to look at the sergeant too, but he subdued the urge, which, surprisingly, allowed him unexpected satisfaction. He then flicked the folded paper, quite stylistically (probably under the influence of Paul Newman), on to the dirt and waited for the man to pick it up. The man did not move. The delight he'd experienced just a moment ago faded.

'Any weapons?'

'No, sir.'

'Strip!'

The man seemed confused. He looked to the sergeant, who was reining in his glee, with a silent request to intervene on behalf of the helpless. Then he looked to the short one, but the stern face, in fact, scared him for the first time.

'But, sir, be reasonable. Habibi, you can check me through my clothes; my son . . .'

'Shut your trap! Do I have to repeat it?'

Silence.

The light breeze stopped again, making everyone intensely aware of the heat.

The man, downcast, reluctantly started taking his shirt off. Below his hairy chest, the protruding belly looked almost comical. The man bent his knees to untie his shoes. He stopped momentarily and implored, 'Sir, for the sake of my son . . .'

'Even a mule is better than you, for it listens!'

Soon the man stood naked with his strong but pudgy body. His face had darkened and eyes grown moist even under the ruthless heat of the day. All his clothes lay in a pile over his beaten leather shoes. The shame he had felt earlier had given way to an impotent rage, and later to resignation. His shoulders stooped beyond their natural capacity. The man had, as if in the passage of humiliation, forgotten his son; but perhaps not. He conceivably felt if he embraced the humiliation, no harm would come to his son, who stood as a mute witness to the theatrics of power.

'Put your filthy underpants on,' the soldier ordered.

The man obeyed once again, ever so grateful. The man whispered *Shukran*! The young reservist squinted his brows; thought he'd heard *Shaitan* instead. His ears turned into molten iron.

'What the fuck did you say?' he yelled in English, unconsciously—quickly pointing his rifle at the man, then lowering it just a tad.

The man answered through his choking voice, 'Thank you, I said, thank you.'

Moazzam Sheikh

So the cunt understands English, the rascal, no, the snake, he corrected himself, that's right.

'Liar, you old snake!'

The man shrugged, as though resigned to the infatuation of the bullet.

He must have cut a hilarious picture with his head bowed, with any kind of stiffness gone from his spine, and the swollen belly, because the sergeant and the shorty burst out laughing almost in sync. Hearing the laughter, the other two rushed out from the office.

Layla, the light of my life! If I kill this man, I'll dedicate it to you, my love! You who thought I was shit, a failed piece of shit. I was nothing; how wrong you were, my Persian pearl, you who still sing nocturnes to my soul, how wrong! I am a contender! Not an ass with big ears but a contender!

His mind began to suck back the elation he had felt earlier and he was pondering over another form of humiliation he could heap on the man and that too before the son (*see, Layla?*) when the sergeant's voice annoyed him:

'Good job, but wrap it up quickly.'

Just then the phone rang. One of them went in to answer it. A laugh was heard outside.

'Who is it, Big D?'

'Mr Saffire,' came the reply. 'He wants to know how the new reservist is doing.'

'Fuck Mr Saffire—well, tell him he's doing fine.'

He tried to refocus; tried to bring all his thinking ability to his aid like a man hanging by a thread.

Just then he remembered the emaciated donkey tied to the pole.

'Okay, you snake, let's cut it short; now listen, you cooperate with me and I let you go,' he proposed in mock friendliness.

The man seemed willing to do anything to have the spell of misery over with. His eyes widened a bit.

'All right, then; go over to your father over there, lift the tail and plant a wet kiss on the asshole like you do in your bedroom.

Make it a bull's eye; no cheating! In return you go home with your son and thank your Allah.'

The man's face flushed with blood and for a moment he could not hear anything.

The soldiers exchanged glances with a mix of surprise and admiration.

The man was brought back to his senses by the soldier's yelling 'Or I'll have to shoot your balls' before he found himself moving voluntarily. The fourth soldier had ended the briefing over the phone and did not want to miss the Oscar-level performance. All five of them watched the man trudge, as if on stage, as slowly as possible, with death written on his back, over to the donkey and then stand still. Their gaze pierced the back of his head.

He closed his eyes for a moment. He opened them slowly, summoning the courage, and lifted the donkey's tail, while fearing a kick in return, but the animal remained calm, not even bothering to shoo the flies away. The man closed his eyes again and brought his lips close to the animal's asshole, to kiss, with the kind of serenity one acquired while offering prayers and remembering God. He paused for a moment. He seemed to check his breath. A pindrop silence. The soldiers too had stopped breathing. Right then another gust of hot wind blew, raising dust and fallen leaves in its mobius ire. The man planted the kiss and slowly leaned back, his head hung low. He remained there, still, as though ashamed to face the world, swallowed by darkness. The soldiers breathed a sigh of relief. Then the short one began giggling, almost in a fit, as if from a deep sense of sadness, which encouraged the others to relax as well. The sergeant clapped, 'Bravo! Bravo! Well done, my Yankee Doodle Dundy.'

'Dandy,' corrected one of the soldiers.

'Shut up.' The giggles died down.

Nothing in the world had prepared anyone, neither the soldiers, nor the chronicler of this tale, above all the sergeant for what they would confront as they turned on hearing a faint sound behind their back. The boy, that little feeble thing they had

Moazzam Sheikh

forgotten, erased from their memory, written him off, that little snake, venom hardening over his pores, the emaciated invisible little man, yes, that half-man had dared grab a piece of rock. The young soldier, the rookie reservist (*the failed American novelist*), was in shock, frozen on a pause button, thinking it to be an act of his imagination. Then, something central stiffened inside him, his eyes bulged, then narrowed, like a hero in a war movie . . . *What we have here is a failure to communicate!* . . . a man rising to occasion, and he slowly raised his rifle, taking an aim at the boy's chest.

'Drop the rock, son,' shouted his father with the ferocity that seemed to have rattled the soldiers' nerves.

The four soldiers, the sergeant, and the helpless father witnessed the boy's stoic face turn igneous, fearless, and the hand holding the rock rise in a gesture of unimaginable defiance to strike at the oppressor of his father and the usurper of his land. It was clear that the innocence of the stone had scared everyone.

papa's girl

Soniah Naheed Kamal

I want my wife's vagina to be smooth like the sides of a banana split in two. I do not like a clothed vagina. It must be stripped, naked and warm. I will shudder at the sight of even a five o'clock shadow. My carnal needs will go unsatisfied and I will be unhappy. My wife stammered with nervousness when I told her what I want. She stammered because she is not a wanton woman, who lie on bed half covered by tattered towels. I am a man who knows what he wants and to hell with nervousness. I have married, and now I will get the wife I have wanted. She is young, and as yet her head is empty of ideas. I will be her idea box. All she knows will come from me. She will be a good wife, for she will have received her training from me. I will shape her into a supine seductress, whose light in life will be to shine on me. Keep me happy on all accounts.

My wife will be happy. She is bound to be. In keeping me happy we will avoid all altercation and this will promote a smiling household fit for the kids I want. I want three. Two boys and one girl. One of the boys is bound to be a wastrel, and so the other will be my support in old age. The daughter will be our breeze. She will breeze from our lives into her husband's, and breeze back and forth to offer daughterly support. Of course our daughter will be both good and beautiful. Of what use is womankind if they cannot boast of beauty?

From *Talus Review*, Spring 2002, Colorado, USA

But, I repeat, for all this the number one factor is a clean vagina. I do not like the thought of blood nor of matted hair—black, blonde, red—since it fills me with distaste so arid that I could waste away like a rice paddy in a desert.

I like rice; polished, white clean grains soft and chewy like my manhood before it rises. I get a rise while eating rice. I think of my lovely wife with her two red lips softly cleaning me. I must not write about it any more. It is too much. I may dream again, and soil my sheets with dreams that I do not like. I am but human, and alas control is not always in my hands. Already I am flushed and a library is hardly a place for lush thoughts. If the librarian happens to see me, hot and sticky, God forbid that she is to think that this is for her. Crass woman with hennaed hair, floppy flesh that looks like a wrinkled Portobello mushroom. Her juices must be dry, and even more dreadful she must be stubbly. She must not take care of her regions. When would she get the time! She is a working woman. Not like my wife will be.

My wife will be at home. She will oversee the domestic chores, which are not many. A steaming meal, one cup tea, starched white shirt for me to wear to the office daily, grey trousers, imitation leather shoes polished, my copy of the *Herald* by my bedside, perhaps a glass of milk if I am in the need; that is all I need. What a simple, luxurious life, the life of my wife. I will not require her to talk to me about anything. She can stay as uninformed as she chooses, and I will teach her to choose to stay that way. I will mould her such that her tragedies will be the death of a plant, her joys my unyielding affection. I will have to watch who she socializes with. But once again, my early training will have taught her that her friends will be fat cats concerned with the cost of cream. They will discuss which pickles we husband folk enjoy, and how they can improve on their preparation. Their joys will be their children, and their woes will be few.

I will bring up the children too. My two sons and one girl. I will spare the rod, but let loose the tongue. They will tremble each time I open my mouth, and bow in deference even when I don't. One son, as I have said, must be allowed to be a wastrel. From my own observation I have gleaned that this forces, as well as encourages the other son not only to fulfil his father's dreams, but also feel obligated to do so.

I will keep the children happy. I guarantee them one trip to the States. Perhaps Disneyland. As they grow they must be able to converse intelligently, and intelligent conversation necessitates one trip abroad. Ho hey, they will say, I am Dada of my domain, I am a great traveller. Once again I quote my own experience. It is not, I say, the quantity of times that one travels; rather it is the quality that one imbues to one's one time. My father took me to Thailand once. Ask those who know me and hear them swear that I have been there at least once every year for the past forty years. It is all in the twist of the tongue, the silvery rattle of the mind. As my mind believes, so my tongue pours. If I were not in control of my senses, I might have started believing that Thailand was indeed a yearly trip.

I met a girl there. In Thailand. I do believe she was Papa's consort. At first I just saw him pinch her buttock. Such a thin buttock she had, but he was able to pinch it greedily. He thought I was too young to have known, but age does not always dictate the extent of knowledge. It is true that I did not know what goes into what, and how many times, but I swear when I saw that pinch I felt a bruise in my heart as cold as an ice-cube pressed against my tongue.

All men are sexual animals; thank God there are women as pure as dew. My wife will be an untarnished creature. She has, but of late, outgrown her knee socks, undone her pigtails and piled up her hair to expose her neck. My wife will never want to be the rascals that some women cannot help but be. Papa's consort, that Thai woman, was older than me and taller as well, although the first time I heard her speak I thought she was a little child, halting and funny.

'Pappu,' she said, 'Have you ever been to Bangkok?'

Dodo-head, I'd replied, I am in Bangkok. I did not think much about it then, but now that Papa is dead I wonder if she was his

Soniah Naheed Kamal

choice, or if feeble minds were all he was able to attract. She was feeble, indeed, but that did not stop her from being a woman.

How should I forget that day when I walked into Papa's small and musty hotel room, our meal from the night before still sitting on the table, alive with putrid fleas, and Dodo-head lying on the bed. Papa had sent me to play. Go play, Papa had said, Here is a dollar, Go get yourself a cola. I came back in tears minutes later, having been robbed by an urchin goon as Papa called them. I found Dodo-head lying on the cigarette-stained hotel sheets, a dirty white towel thrown over her waist and one breast. Such a small, flat breast like a sliver of smoked salmon. I had gone in to find Papa, but instead I found the sight of black hair dribbling from between her legs. A cinder valley, neither open nor shut. Her eyes were closed and she did not hear me come in. I heard Papa pull the toilet flush and panic stricken I hid behind the heavy curtains. They stunk of stale sunlight, and when Papa came out he looked white and flabby like unfried fish. My mother used to make the best fried fish in the world before she burnt up in the kitchen, and died. Kerosene, bah! We've been using a gas stove ever since.

Papa waddled over to the bed, and farting, lay next to her. She opened her eyes, and I could taste her silly sigh. Her father was a fisherman and everything about Dodo-head smelled like baby shrimps in brine. Her hand was like a lever, the more Papa stroked it the wider her legs opened. I could not close my eyes. I tried. Now I know that it was the shock of seeing a woman naked, but back then I had thought that Dodo-head was a witch whose black hairs, spewing between her legs like stiff seaweed, had cast a spell over me. Papa did not seem to have a problem with her hair. He lifted it out of the way, as if it were a veil that needed but dislodging.

I want my wife to be without veil. I do not want me to be caught in her hair as Papa was caught. It was so messy. I felt bad for Papa. Cleanliness is next to Godliness. I even carry a bathroom roll with me and wipe everything many a time before touching it. I would admonish Papa whenever he sat on a rickshaw seat without wiping it first, or passed by a dust bunny without shuddering. How Papa could just lift her hair and coax his face between her legs as if he were thirsty and she the cleanest cesspool, I will never know. Actually in my dreams, it is not Papa I see for his face is hidden in Dodo-head's furry nether, it is she I see instead. It is her face that stares unabashed in dusty sunlight leaking through metal screens. It is her eyelashes that move up and down as rapidly as Papa's head. Her black eyelashes, figments of that which Papa had lifted out of his way.

Life has enough obstacles to offer an ambitious man; I want a wife who understands the necessity for removal as well as prefers a cool, temperate climate, as do I, so that she won't be sticky and dripping as she had been when she had gotten up. She and Papa had left the bedroom for a cold drink. I had wanted to accompany them for I was as hot and sick of the summer as they must have been. My wife will learn to loathe summer sweat as much as I do, for I will be an able teacher. I will teach her all that is in my power and beyond. I will show her what the good life is all about, but she must first show me that she deserves my efforts. She must be clean. She must be shorn. She must be as silky as satin. She must come to me as Dodo-head never came to Papa.

I saw her daily the two weeks we tanned in Thailand. Papa was in the dark even until he died, but she I think knew that I knew. She said such shameful things to me and she would peep at the curtains, as if I had invented the art of ogling.

'What do you want Dodo-head?' I had boldly ventured one day when Papa left the two of us alone in his room.

'Do you want what you saw?' she asked licking the drool that always seeped out of her mouth.

'I saw nothing.'

'You saw all. Come, is this what you saw? Touch. The Papa will not know. We will not tell The Papa. Touch. Touch. Why you no touch? You no like?'

Soniah Naheed Kamal

'Is Papa's!' I said rearing back from her gaping legs. I had wanted to say that it smelled of dried brine on a hot rock. That the summer sun had matted it into unclean bands of black hair and pink shrimpy flesh.

'Touch like so,' she coaxed as she coiled around my unwilling fingers.

'Please let me go,' I whimpered, my hand caught in her thick mesh.

'You foolish,' she giggled, 'You no have to pay. I give to you for free. Now you touch. Hey, where you going?'

I had run away. Ashamed with fright and equally ashamed that I was frightened. I was frightened that I would lose control, that she would teach me something I would be unwilling to learn.

I want a wife who has nothing to teach. I will not tolerate being taught. I want a woman who stays in her place; if I wanted a Dodo-head I could have paid for one. I could have had one for free.

***

Today my wife lies on our nuptial bed atop a brocade of carnations. She is as yellow with turmeric baths as sunflowers roasted in the sun. I am sitting on my high chair, drinking a glass of milk for tonight I am in need. This is my first night, and I am agog with anticipation. I was not allowed to inspect the softness of my wife to be! What hypocrisy I had thought. I had told her what I expected and she had told me that she had duly complied. Yet I had not been allowed to taste a feel. I would have taught her how to let me cruise my fingers around her, but her father had been in the room. His face was as grim as mine when Papa would pretend that Dodo-head was just a good friend. The soles of my wife's feet are oiled and glossy. I think of Dodo-head's feet and grow quite angry at my lack of control at banishing her from my mind. Here is my wife, ready to be inspected by me, and I am thinking of Dodo-head's cracked heels, her toenails as grey as a cardboard shark? I get up and tersely tell my wife to open her eyes. She is never to shut her eyes, I teach her. I tell her about girls who close their eyes and flutter their eyelashes. She is scared that she has displeased me. I know by the way she jolts her eyes open, kohl black, as black as Dodo-head's hair. Shut them, I say, angry now that even her dreamy eyes remind me of Dodo-head. I decide it is time I act and not instruct, so I plunge my finger into the flesh of her ankle. She stiffens as I grope past her calf and up her thigh. This pleases me for Dodo-head was never shy. My fingers slow down now because I do not want to find out what I can already smell. She is thick with salt that gathers under a heavy garment after a humid day of wedding ceremony. My fingers collide with her bare skin. My wife's nether is as plump as a lychee. But she is cold, and on her dehaired parts little goosebumps gather like raindrops on a waxed window. Unbidden Dodo-head's long mesh pricks my fingertips, and my fingers recoil. I think of me behind a curtain, of Papa, of Dodo-head who smelled like fresh water shrimp. I think of my wife and everything I have to teach her. I have to teach her patience and abstinence. I pat her and turn to sleep. She will have much to do in the mornings to come, for I know that in the mornings she will wash my slippery sheet, polished wet with dreams of Dodo-head. With too many dreams of Dodo-head.

Soniah Naheed Kamal

the door is open

Zubair Ahmed

First, the dream.

The same old house, our house—in Krishan Nagar.

I wonder how long the dreams of the house will haunt me.

The teeny, old room of mine. Midnight. I have been reading Bedi's stories. All my life, I have loved them, though I never seem to overcome one line: 'When we are with one friend, why then do we still long for a second one?' I marvel at the beautiful thought and how well it is expressed. On the slightest noise, I go to the window. Three friends await me in the alley below. One of them stands in the moonlight; his face breaks into a smile on seeing me. The other one is half in the moonlight and half in darkness. I recognize him too; he adjusts his glasses with his hand and clears his throat. The third one is completely obscured by darkness. I can only take a shot in the dark; but a guess, you know, is always a guess. The first one, who is smiling, squeaks aloud, 'Hey man, he'd come to see us; our pull brought him here. Now he thinks we should do something.' I am still under the spell of Bedi's words: 'When we are with one friend, why do we still long for a second one?' I too feel delighted to see him, mingled with the bliss I derive from Bedi's pondering. I say, 'Step in.' But, wait, let me sketch the entire map. I have remained trapped in it all my life.

Originally published as 'Buha Khulla Aye' in *Meenh, Boohe te Barrian*, Rut Lekha Publications, 2001, Lahore

Imagine a two-storey house. My uncle used to live downstairs and we upstairs. There are two rooms up here. You entered the house by first entering the foyer, and then to the right, no, to the left were the stairs. After climbing up eight to ten steps—Ah, well, I have gone up and down those steps for twenty-one years, but now I seem to have forgotten—all right, all right, let's say ten to twelve steps (I'll ask Taqi, since he's always musing over the house); so there, after going up eight to ten steps, to your left, opens a door into a big room. Look, I forget again. No, there were no windows or doors, just frames in the walls. After evicting us, we heard, my uncle repaired the house and later, adding doors and windows, sold it. Anyway, my mother and brothers shared the room. Then, a little farther ahead as the passage narrows, again to the left, there was a smaller room, which we refer to as the 'gallery'. I have another uncle, and if he heard me speak of it now, he'd be really amused, but, alas, he's not alive anymore.

So that used to be my room. Although one would think it was on the second floor, it was quite close to the street level. You could stand in the window and chat with a person down in the street without any sweat. Right next to the window there was a roof-like increment. The whole problem was a result of this protrusion. Then, there was a piece of land beside our house. Although the plot was empty, it had four walls around it. (The plot isn't empty now; a three-storey building has been constructed there.)

The moment I am about to relate here belongs to the time when there was nothing there. But now even the street has changed. Moreover, we are talking dreams here!

Anyway, you could easily talk to the person standing just below the window. So I tell the first friend, 'Climb right in.' He climbs up the wall in a jiffy, walks across the protrusion, and he's right there, where I am. He hops in through the window and into my room. There are still two more friends at the door. The second one, who is half in darkness and half in light, adjusts his glasses and grumbles, suggesting he wants me to come down and open the door. He has no inclination to perform scaling-the-

Zubair Ahmed

wall and walking-the-protrusion acrobatics. I'd feared just that. All my life, I've feared that and now even in my dream I am scared. But who is going to open the door? I have already told you my uncle lives downstairs.

Since childhood we have lived under the constant tyranny of my uncle. Though we lived upstairs, we lived in dread. If we dropped something unintentionally, he'd roar from downstairs, 'Can't you sit in peace, you dogs? Why raise hell? First, I give you a place to live, then I have to put up with your monkey business.' From childhood to adulthood, this fear climbed to coldly sit atop our being and manifested itself deep within our features. For twenty years he stood with his heel pressed down on us. Dread left its enduring dent on our faces, while fear sculpted our entire life. So who's going to open the door? Since I was the oldest among the brothers, I inherited a bigger share of it. I have wrestled with it for a big part of my life. I feel an intense urge to go and open the door though. All my life I have been longing to open closed doors. I am grown up now. The fear too has ebbed, but not vanished completely. Don't know if my friends know this— the ones who are still standing in the street and the one who has climbed in, scaling the wall and walking across the protrusion.

Two friends still remain at the door. Scared and unsure of how to proceed and open the door, I remember Bedi's line again, 'When we are with one friend, why do we still long for a second one?' But Bedi could have said a third friend as well. The fact, however, is that Bedi never said anything about this anywhere. All of this belongs to the realm of dreams. When you cannot even open the door, why does he then insist on coming through the very thing? Why doesn't he simply climb the wall and walk across to come inside? I have already invited him in a couple times. But he didn't give me an answer. He is just like that. I am certain he'll continue standing there for the rest of his life and I by the window. The one who's already in, says in his ever-typical manner, 'Come on . . . what's your problem?' I remain next to the window; the other one is still down there, beside the one who's engulfed by darkness; always hiding his body; always staying behind . . . fear, no, no. I think of my uncle again. Suddenly I feel it is nothing. I can go downstairs and open the door. It seems to me that the yearning to see friends is greater than fear. The yearning engulfs fear, which in my case has completely evaporated.

Then, all of a sudden I open my eyes. The crows are raising hell. The picture of the old neighbourhood drifts past my eyes. It's been twenty-one years since we left that house and the neighbourhood.

It's morning. A faint light has crept into the room through the window. It seems as though fear has climbed down the stairs and longing has climbed up instead. Just like the twittering of sparrows has gradually overcome and perched atop the crow's cawing. I look as I leave the room and find the door surprisingly open. Well, why don't you come in!

—*Translated from the Punjabi by Moazzam Sheikh*

Zubair Ahmed

if truth be told

Javed Shaheen

The bus slowed down, then stopped with a jolt. The conductor, who had been dozing, popped his eyes open, looked groggily at the passengers, who had been dozing as well, and said in a sleepy voice, 'Passengers for Chawk Garh Maharaja, this is your stop.'

He repeated his call a few times. Some peasant men and women picked up their bundles and got off the bus. The conductor looked through the bus again, walked over to Ahmad, shook him by the shoulder and said, 'Bao-ji, this is Chawk Garh Maharaja!'

Ahmad started. He couldn't remember when he had dozed off. He knew he had been awake when the bus reached Trimu Irrigation Headworks, and later when it pulled into Atthara Hazari. After that he had no recollection. He had succumbed to sleep. He hurriedly picked up his overnight bag and got off the bus.

Outside he looked at his watch. It was six-thirty in the morning. It was a beautiful morning in March. The chill still hung in the air and stung whenever the wind blew. He regretted not bringing along a sweater. He sat down on the dirt ridge running along the edge of a field by the roadside. The dull, sluggish feeling that follows interrupted sleep clung to him. The glow of the rising sun was spreading slowly over the neighbouring wheat fields, where the spikes had already sprouted but were

Originally published as 'Aik Haqeeqat Ka Aetraaf' in *Savera*, Fall Issue, 2000, Lahore still green, and the grain inside hadn't fully matured. Tahili trees ran along both sides of the road, forming a long arch. Nearby was a tonga stand and a few shops which were still closed. Only the shop that fixed bicycle flats was open. Another establishment, which looked like a restaurant and lodging, was just opening. Outside it, a man was trying to get the stove going.

By now Ahmad had shaken off both his sleep and his sluggishness and was waiting for the restaurant to open so that he could get some breakfast. Meanwhile a couple of buses had pulled up, dropped off some passengers and gone off again. When he noticed the proprietor put the kettle on, he got up and walked over to him. The man invited him to sit inside.

The restaurant was fairly spacious and was scattered with a few wooden tables and chairs. The place hadn't been cleaned yet. It looked as though it had been left in the mess it was in at closing time the night before.

Spotting a washbasin against a wall, Ahmad took out a toothbrush and paste from his bag and started to brush his teeth.

'Bao-ji, shall I fix you some breakfast?' the man by the stove asked.

He ordered toast, fried eggs, and tea and went back to brushing. By now he could feel pressure building in his bowels. He asked the proprietor for the toilet, and the latter pointed towards the staircase. When Ahmad returned downstairs, a car stopped in front of the restaurant. Three men got out and walked inside. One of them went over and ordered breakfast, then joined his companions who had taken seats around a table. Just then a boy in his mid-teens dashed in and hurriedly started wiping the chairs and tables.

'Where were you?' the man at the stove yelled.

'I overslept, Ustad-ji,' the boy replied softly.

'Must have been hanging out at Gama's shop again last night, watching some film,' the man yelled again. 'Bastard! You can't shake off your bad habits, can you?'

'No, Ustad-ji, no,' the boy pleaded, as he continued wiping. 'It wasn't like that at all.'

Javed Shaheen

'Hurry up! Don't you see Babu-log are waiting.'

The boy began wiping even more energetically.

'How far is Hazrat Sultan Bahu's shrine from here?' Ahmad asked the proprietor as he waited to be served.

'Six, maybe seven miles. Why, are you going there?'

'Yes,' he answered tersely.

The proprietor told him that the tongas would start operating shortly.

One of the three newcomers, who couldn't help overhearing this exchange, addressed Ahmad, saying, 'We're going there too. You can come along with us if you like.'

He felt immensely relieved: that was one problem out of the way! He scrutinized the men. They wore salwar kameez, and from the way they talked appeared to be small-time businessmen. After finishing his breakfast he went over to their table. They came from Faisalabad, he found out in the course of the conversation, and were on their way to Leiah. Since they were in the area, they had decided to stop off and pay a visit to the shrine of Sultan Bahu. Later, driving with them to the shrine, Ahmad gathered that they were contractors for the collection of tolls levied by the Municipal Committee on the movement of goods from one city to another. They were going to Leiah in connection with their work. When they asked Ahmad about himself, he said that he was a state employee in Lahore who had come, as they had, to pay a visit to the shrine of Sultan Bahu.

The truth, however, was quite different. He had never felt inclined to visit and make petitionary prayers at saints' tombs. Even in Lahore, he had never bothered to visit Data Darbar or, for that matter, any other saint's shrine, not because he considered such things heretical but because he was secular in his thinking.

The reason behind his visit to a shrine now was that his mother had left his house twenty days ago and despite extensive search hadn't been found. Every three or four months, she would come from her village to spend a few days at his place. Touchy and irritable by nature, she would squabble over matters of little importance with either his wife or him, take offence, and leave, for her village or her daughter's home in Okara swearing that she would never set foot in his house again. This had happened countless times. Nonetheless, the old lady would eventually return, the whole incident forgotten, or he would go and pay her a visit, and she would remember nothing of what had happened.

It was no different this time. When he returned from work his wife told him that Mother had got into an argument with her and left, declaring, as usual, that she was not coming back, and even went as far as to say, 'Next time my son sees me, he'll be looking at my dead body.' He knew Mother was to blame for most of these tiffs so he didn't ask for details and retired to his room quietly. He telephoned Okara in the evening, but his sister told him that Mother hadn't shown up there. The next day he sent the servant to her village to inquire about her. She wasn't there either. His father came back with the servant. His anxiety mounted. She could not possibly have gone anywhere but to one of these two places.

All of a sudden he remembered how much his mother loved to visit saints' shrines, and this put his mind somewhat at ease. On several occasions she had spent weeks at a time at the shrines of Shabaz Qalandar, Baba Farid Ganj-e Shakar, Baba Bullhe Shah, Data Ganj-Bakhsh, Bibi Pak-Daman, Hazrat Mian Mir, and Sultan Bahu. She had become great friends with several women attached to those shrines. She was especially close to a woman at Hazrat Sultan Bahu's shrine, where she would inevitably stay for a week. Together she and this woman would dole out free food to visitors at the shrine. They had even declared themselves foster sisters.

After a week, when there had been no news of her, he took leave from work and set out in search of her. He looked for her in all the shrines in Lahore. She wasn't there. He did find out, though, that the malangs who were permanent fixtures at these sanctuaries did know his mother. Next he went to the shrines of Baba Bullhe Shah, Farid Ganj-e Shakar, and finally to Shabaz

Qalandar's. When he described his mother to people there, they all seemed to know her. Every year or two she visited the place. But she hadn't come this year, he was told. Only Sultan Bahu's shrine remained. He was positive he would find his mother there, or at least some trace of her. He boarded the one o'clock bus bound for Darya Khan and got off in the morning at Chawk Garh Maharaja.

The dome of the shrine appeared in the distance. They arrived shortly and the car came to a stop. They got out and strode to the shrine's front entrance, where they took off their shoes, and stepped inside the courtyard, proceeding towards the tomb chamber. More than half the courtyard was filled with people. Quranic recitation on loudspeakers was in progress, which, his companions informed him, never stopped.

After circling the tomb, they took a moment to join their hands in prayer. Afterwards, each put a sum of money in the donation box at the head of the tomb. Soon the three men were ready to depart. Ahmad, however, said that he wished to stay longer, and shaking hands with them, walked inside

In the time it took him to circumambulate the tomb in the big hall and offer his supplication, his lungs had filled with the heady perfume of aloes wood and incense and he stepped into the courtyard to get some fresh air. He walked for a while along the side that was relatively shaded and then sat down. The sun was shining brightly and had flooded the entire courtyard. It was Friday. Large flocks of visitors, most of them peasant men and women, had been streaming in since the morning. Their worn and dirty clothes bespoke their poverty, and their sunken cheeks and the sadness in their faces revealed the melancholy tenor of their existence. They had come to Sultan Bahu seeking some release from their oppressive lives, some comfort for their troubled hearts. Ahmad had observed people crying inconsolably and making abject entreaties as if a shrine was the only place left for them to turn to. They would remove their few coins tied up in the ends of their torn dupattas or dingy turbans and put them reverentially in the collection boxes. Some who themselves had difficulty making ends meet were feeding the useless bunch of idlers who hung around these shrines. What a cruel business! Who would make their wishes come true? Hear their prayers? They were illuminating Sultan Bahu's darbar—but who would light their own homes? A wave of anguish shot through him.

Meanwhile the sunlight had inched its way to his resting place. He got up. He had to look for Mai Allah Rakkhi, the friend his mother stayed with during her visits here. He moved about in the courtyard. The recitation of the Holy Book was still going on. Suddenly his eyes fell on a malang in a green robe. He looked like one of the shrine's residents. Ahmad strode over to him, his heart pounding, and asked him about Mai Allah Rakkhi.

'Of course she's here,' the malang said. 'Come with me, I'll take you to her.' He gestured for Ahmad to follow. They walked to the far corner of the courtyard, where the malang stopped in front of a cell. The door was latched from the outside.

'This is her place,' the malang said. 'You stay here while I go look for her.' He went back to the yard and disappeared in the milling crowd.

Having barely slept the night before, Ahmad was overcome with fatigue. He sat down on a platform nearby, taking his bag off his shoulder and laying it down near his feet. His eyes had begun to close with the onslaught of sleep. Just then the malang reappeared, with a woman in tow.

'This is Mai Allah Rakkhi,' he said, approaching Ahmad.

The woman, a tall, spare figure, gave Ahmad a penetrating look. She was about seventy and had a tawny complexion, bulging eyes and a sharp nose. She unfastened the latch and he followed her inside. The malang left them, crying, 'Ya Bahu! Ya Bahu!'

A mat with a cotton quilt on it was spread out on one side in the cell, and Ahmad made himself comfortable here.

'Son, what brings you to me?' she asked him after he sat down.

'Mai-ji, I'm Sardari Begum's son. You know her, don't you?'

'Why, of course, my son. She's my adopted sister.'

'Mai-ji, she left the house twenty days ago. I came to see whether she is with you.'

'Son, she comes here all the time and stays for several days each time. If you ask me, she's a fakir at heart. This is where her heart is, not with her family. But for some reason she hasn't shown up yet this year. I think about her every day.'

Ahmad's heart sank. His last thread of hope had snapped. What more did he need to know?

Mai Allah Rakkhi, continued, 'She does everything with such love and devotion when she's here. Together we sweep the courtyard and distribute food to the visitors. She likes it here so much that she won't leave—I have to send her away. I reason with her, "Look, Sardari, you've got children and even grandchildren. They need you. Go to them. If you leave them and stay here, God won't be pleased with you. You've earned true fakiri, even as you live and work in this world. Just pray for your family's well-being when you come here. You mustn't renounce the world. It will hurt your children." '

The woman's voice seemed to be coming from far away. She stopped and stared at his face. He told her the places he'd gone to in search of his mother before he had come here. This brought an expression of concern to the old lady's face.

'How terribly sad!' she said, breaking her silence. 'She used to visit all the other darbars as well and tell me about them. Sometimes she would ask me to come along to visit them. But how can I leave this place? I have a particularly demanding job. I've got to take care of practically all the chores, and above all, Hazrat Sultan Bahu is especially kind to me.' After a brief pause, she continued, 'But where has Sardari Bibi gone? Why is she putting her children through so much trouble? For the sake of Hazrat Sultan Bahu, may she be well wherever she is.'

Silence prevailed for a few minutes inside the dim cell. Then she asked, 'Shall I get you something to eat, my son? The langar must be ready now.'

'No, Mai-ji. I had breakfast at Chawk Garh Maharaja. But I've been travelling the whole night and would like to rest for a while. Would it be all right for me to take a nap here?'

'Certainly, son. By all means. Let me fix the bed properly for you. Sleep for as long as you like, I won't bother you. I'm off to the langar.' She got up and left, closing the door behind her.

He stretched out on the quilt. His mother's face stayed in his mind for a while and then he dozed off. When he got up it was around three in the afternoon. He had been asleep for a long time and had to leave now, he thought. When he opened the door, he found Mai Allah Rakkhi sitting on the low wall at the edge of the courtyard. The minute she saw him, she said, 'You were asleep, my son. I didn't wish to disturb you, so I decided to sit outside. I've brought you food. Go back in. I'll bring it right away.'

She went to one side and returned with a few rotis and some daal. By now Ahmad was quite hungry. But the shock of not having found his mother dampened his appetite. He felt terribly depressed. When Mai Allah Rakkhi saw his condition, she tried to comfort him, 'Don't be sad, my son. Your mother will certainly come back. Of that I'm sure. Why would she want to hurt you? If she comes here, I'll personally bring her to you. Don't worry. I won't let her go anywhere else. Now, here, eat your food.'

She took out a bowl and filled it with daal and laid out the rotis on a handkerchief. Ahmad sat down on the quilt and started to eat. Meanwhile Mai Allah Rakkhi continued: 'God knows where she's wandered off to! May He keep her well! May Sultan Bahu keep her in his protection! My heart tells me that she will definitely come back. Don't you worry, son . . .'

A while later, Ahmad found himself outside the front entrance. A few tongas stood a short distance away. He got into the one bound for Chawk Garh Maharaja.

As soon as the tonga started he lit a cigarette, his second since morning. But a few puffs later his thoughts had returned to his mother. He felt totally crestfallen that he had not found her at the shrine. He had pinned all his hopes on this place. How would he face his father? The poor old man, how miserable he'd feel. His father had tried to insist on coming with him; only after much pleading had he been able to talk him out of it. The old couple lived in the village. Each was the other's greatest support. Even though his mother was haughty and the two had difficulty getting along, they took care of each other. How would his father manage now? How would he live all by himself in the village? Who would watch over him? At such an advanced age the departure of one partner usually . . . The very thought made him shudder.

It had always bothered him that his father had become so used to living in the village that it was impossible to get him out of it. Whenever he had to spend a few days in Lahore, he couldn't wait to go back. Travel was such an ordeal for him. After his retirement he'd had a tubewell dug on the cultivable stretch of the land he owned. He'd planted a large orchard of mangoes, oranges, guavas, and jamans next to the well, and lived a contented life there.

His elder brother and sister had looked at him with such scorn in their eyes, as though he were to blame for her disappearance. Everybody was constantly badgering his wife about it: What happened? What caused the tiff? After all, would Mother take such a serious step without a good reason? People just don't walk away from their comfortable homes for no reason at all, do they? His wife was beginning to feel like a criminal. She swore to everyone that the squabble was far from being serious enough to provoke such a drastic reaction: as usual, the minute she'd arrived from the village the old lady had started chiding her, 'You won't let my son's household prosper!' Ahmad's wife had asked repeatedly, 'What woman doesn't want her own house to prosper?' Moreover, whatever she bought, she bought with her husband's endorsement. But the old lady refused to see it that way. Finally, fed up, his wife had invited her to move in with them for good and take charge of the expenses. This wasn't such a big thing, was it?

The tonga was moving along at a steady speed. They had covered half the distance already. The sun was shining less fiercely now, and there was an exquisite aroma rising from the wheat fields on either side of the road. The sky was perfectly clear and the breeze was pleasantly cool. Perched on his front seat, the coachman was humming away, absorbed in his thoughts. Now and then he whipped the horse out of sheer habit. Suddenly he threw a question at him: 'Bao-ji, what do you think, will Bhutto Sahib's life be spared, or will they hang him?'

He thought for a few seconds. He had no interest in politics, and he had not given the matter any thought. His silence prompted the coachman to repeat his question, 'Tell me, Bao-ji. A terrible injustice, wouldn't you say?'

'It's hard to be sure. These are government affairs,' Ahmad said dismissively, to get him out of his hair. The coachman got the message. He returned to his humming.

The clip-clop of the horse's hooves rose distinctly from the road. Farmers' mud houses, studded with cowdung cakes that had been slapped on the walls to dry, were seen on either side. Farther on, the tonga came to a stretch of road that was pitted in places, causing the horse to slow down.

He would reach Chawk Garh Maharaja by five-thirty, he thought. And if he were lucky and caught the bus soon enough, he might reach Lahore by midnight. Part of him was also wondering whether he should perhaps go to Okara instead, via Jhang and Sahiwal, to inform his sister about the developments and plan his next move. But he quickly abandoned the idea. For one thing, it would prolong his journey needlessly, and for another, his father would be expecting him in Lahore. But what did he have to tell him, really? Where else should he look for his mother? Where might she be at the moment? And in what state? His head was filled with confusion. All of a sudden the proverbial bond of motherly love and affection had begun to look very tenuous indeed. Where had Mother disappeared to, throwing the entire family into this endless torment? This sort of thing could be the bane of one's whole life!

Javed Shaheen

Twilight was spreading by the time he reached Chawk Garh Maharaja and got out of the tonga. He stood by the edge of the road to wait for a bus to Lahore. But suddenly, he changed his mind. He didn't feel like setting out again so soon. He still hadn't recovered from the exhaustion of the first trip. He walked towards the restaurant where he had eaten his breakfast in the morning. Abbas, the proprietor, recognized him right away and said, 'Bao-ji, so you've paid your visit to the darbar?'

'Yes,' he replied and then asked him if there was a room to spend the night.

'We've got three rooms upstairs. Visitors to the darbar who arrive late in the day stay with us.'

He led Ahmad upstairs and showed him the rooms. Two were large and had three or four cots each. The third was small with only two cots, but had an attached bathroom. Ahmad preferred the latter and asked, 'What's the price?'

'Twenty rupees,' Abbas said.

'All right then. Make it ready.'

'Please take a seat downstairs. I'll take care of everything.'

Leaving his bag in the room, Ahmad went downstairs and left the restaurant. Darkness was spreading rapidly, and the air had become chilly. He walked some distance and then stopped to watch the people getting on and off the buses. Lights had come on in the few shops nearby. The town of Garh Maharaja was up ahead. He thought of going there for a while, but then decided against it.

He felt chilly and returned to the restaurant. Meanwhile Abbas had readied the room. He had laid out fresh bedsheets and a quilt which looked clean enough. Ahmad examined the bathroom. It too looked clean.

'Bao-ji, we know just what our customers want!' Abbas remarked, noticing that he seemed satisfied with the room. 'If you need anything, just ring,' he said, pointing at the bell.

Just then Ahmad heard children's voices coming from the room next door. Abbas told him it was a family from

Rawalpindi—husband, wife and two children. They'd come to the shrine to give thanks as one of their wishes had been fulfilled.

Since he had eaten very little of the food Mai Allah Rakkhi had brought him that afternoon, he was famished. He closed the door and went downstairs. Abbas recited the menu and he selected a vegetable dish and some rotis. After the meal he lit a cigarette and stayed at the table until he had finished smoking. He was enjoying being away from the commotion of the bustling city and his friends. He suddenly felt incredibly free! If only he could spend a few more days in such freedom! Humans fashion their own shackles! And their own prisons as well!

He returned to his room and opened the only window that overlooked the street. He peered into the darkness. The tonga stand was empty and most of the shops had also closed for the day. He looked at his watch. It was almost nine o'clock. A gust of wind fluttered the pages of an old calendar that hung on the wall behind him. He remained standing at the window, peering into the darkness outside. The window of the next room was six feet away, and he could hear the voices of the Rawalpindi family clearly. A child was whining, pestering his mother to tell a story. Groggily the mother was telling him to go to sleep. But the child was insistent. Ahmad then remembered his own childhood. He too used to pester his mother for stories at bedtime. She had told him all the stories she knew about jinns, fairies, and princesses. Indeed she had recounted them several times. There was one story in particular which he never seemed to tire of: 'Ma! tell me that story. The one about Nana Abbu, when he ran into a witch . . .'

'I've told it twenty times already. Let it be, won't you?' she'd say, feeling tired and irritated.

'No, Ma, just one more time, please,' he'd beg her.

'All right,' she'd start. 'Your grandpa was a tehsildar. One day a messenger visited him in the evening and said that the Deputy Commissioner wanted to see him about some important matter. He was to be at his bungalow at eight in the morning. The city was some thirty miles from your grandpa's tehsil. There weren't cars and trains back in those days. People travelled on horseback. Since it was a long journey, your grandpa saddled the horse and set out that very evening.'

At this point he'd look closely at his mother. This was where the action started! 'What happened next, Ma?' he'd ask, rapt with interest.

'First get me a glass of water.'

He'd dash off to do it.

'Well now . . . what was I saying?'

'That Nana Abbu set out that very evening.'

'Oh, yes. So he set out that very evening. It wasn't as populated as it is today. Roads used to be quite desolate. There was even a jungle on the way. As your grandpa was passing through it, he heard a woman crying. Then she appeared and started to run alongside your grandpa's horse, begging him to let her ride with him, because she was terribly tired from walking for such a long time. Your grandpa, however, didn't answer her and rode on. The horse was getting out of control, as it reared in agitation.'

'Whatever for, Ma?'

'Because she wasn't a real woman. She was actually a witch in the guise of a woman. And horses, you must know, are benevolent spirits. They can recognize evil spirits right away. Anyway, your grandpa's horse began to neigh loudly. Meanwhile the woman kept begging to be allowed to mount the horse. Your grandpa turned a deaf ear and continued riding, while she kept running alongside the horse. Your grandpa was a truly brave man. Anyone else in his place would have lost his wits and fainted.'

'But, Ma, it's just as likely that she was a real woman who had lost her way,' he'd cut in. 'She just wanted Grandpa to give her a ride.'

'No, no!' his mother would say emphatically. 'This was no woman. Your grandpa had seen that her feet were turned backwards, and her hair was so long it reached her ankles.'

'Was she pretty, Ma?' he'd ask eagerly.

If Truth Be Told {35}

'Where did you ever hear of witches being pretty?'

'What happened then?'

'Well, she managed to keep up with the horse. She'd cry, then laugh, begging him all the while to let her ride with him. Your grandpa refused to respond to any of her entreaties. Finally, at the break of dawn she cursed your grandpa and ran off, disappearing into the jungle.'

'Ma, why didn't Grandpa let her ride with him? Poor woman, she must've been terribly tired.' His grandpa's hard-heartedness seemed to bother him.

'Fool! No sane person would allow a witch to ride with him!'

'Why not, Ma?'

'That's enough. Go to sleep now! I'm feeling very sleepy. I can't answer your foolish questions.'

She'd turn over in the bed and try to fall asleep. Meanwhile he would think: If only he had been riding behind his grandfather on the horse! At least he could have seen what a churail looked like. Timidly he'd ask, 'Ma, where have churails disappeared to now?'

'In those days it was just wilderness; it's different today with the development of cities and towns. Maybe they've hidden themselves in the jungles. Okay, go to bed now. Don't ruin my sleep. Once something gets into your head, it just won't leave.'

He'd shrink back, defeated, unable to find the courage to ask her any more questions, and at some point he would fall asleep.

Ahmad had been standing at the window for quite a while and could feel the heaviness of sleep in his eyes. He moved to the bed, pulled the quilt over him and sat with his back against the wall. The open window had let the evening chill into the room. It was quiet in the room next door. Perhaps the child had fallen asleep without his mother telling him a story.

Ahmad sat leaning against the wall, deep in thought: In the past ten days he had searched for his mother in every conceivable place he thought she might be. At least now nobody could say that he hadn't looked enough, or had been negligent. But deep down he knew that he had made this enormous effort to find her to satisfy the world, his relatives, his conscience. The truth was that he had never loved his mother in the way a son should. The two were not close, and the roots of their alienation extended deep into the past. What bothered him especially was that his mother had never tried to find out why things had become so cold between them either. From his earliest childhood he had seen his mother only as an imposing, headstrong woman who always wanted to have her way. His father, too, was repressed by her, which made Ahmad even angrier with her. And what upset him the most was the fact that she wanted to run his house completely. She would constantly carp at his wife and even taunt her for coming from a poor family. If he intervened, she would let him have it too. The biggest problem, though, was that his children used to witness this. They were bound to be affected. And this made him extremely unhappy.

She was no different in her daughter's home. She could never get along with her son-in-law. Whenever she was there, she would interfere in their personal matters, and of course it was only natural for her son-in-law to be displeased. If anyone tried to stop her, she'd curse them, pack her belongings, and leave. In the village, she would unleash her wrath on her husband. At harvest time, she'd dole out a bagful of grain to anyone who showed up, not caring about what her husband said.

Almost everyone was unhappy and fed up with her. And yet nobody could muster the courage to let her know it. Now that she was gone, everyone was anxious. That was natural. But deep inside everyone was also feeling tremendously relieved.

A wave of tranquillity swept over his heart. He had admitted a bitter truth. He felt incredibly light, as though a big weight had been lifted off his mind and body at last. And not knowing when, he fell asleep.

—*Translated from the Urdu by Muhammad Umar Memon*

barriers that remained

Vali Ram Vallabh

It had been pouring since the morning; the rain, thick sheets of water. She remained sitting inside her house; didn't go anywhere. Nor could she have. When the miserable rains come knocking, they ignite a fire in your heart. The streets suddenly are full of potholes; water collects in them. Her heart, too, was dotted with them, holding the water of memories; countless events, stories had come to float there. Wounds had opened, pain emerged. She tried to rein in her heart; tried to set up dams around it lest it too might just float away. Although her hands were busy performing chores, she was answering questions, was asking questions. But it wasn't *she*.

For she had died by drowning herself in the whirlpool of the past.

The husband was an officer.

Went away in his car.

The children were of school-going age.

The bus came, and off they went.

She took a deep breath. Now she was alone, quite free despite being enclosed in her fortress-like bungalow, but the rain had erected a wall around the four sides of the fortress and the bungalow got soaked standing like a crane in a state of melancholy. It didn't leak from anywhere; nor was it moist any

Originally published as 'Haden Jo Phlaangi Na Ja Sakeen' in *Zindagi Se Kata Hua Tukra*, Scheherzad Publishers, 2001, Karachi place. The blue colour too hadn't peeled off . . . like a wet cloth. The leaves, flowers, and branches swayed in the garden; all had been washed clean, softened. Not a speck of dust anywhere, nor any trace of patterns etched in mud but . . .

The rain had pulled off the sheet covering her. And it had drenched the other sheet, the sheet of honour.

She had dressed up to go: sweater, scarf, gloves, socks, sandals, overcoat, yet she was naked still; shivering. Then a struggle began between her existence and her heart. There was no visitor. Nor had she been invited anywhere. Not even a message.

No one had phoned.

Today, something should happen today.

An accident from the past, needed to be tossed into her present.

Accidents.

Telegram.

Illness.

Shadows began to stretch. He'll come soon; followed by the children. She'll come to life again.

But when evening comes, it comes to say farewell, not like a woman, who, willing or not, for the rest of her life laughs and weeps while dissolving into silence. Evening leaves, leaving her space for night. It is not a life sentence—one sole relationship, against will, violence. No difference, no change.

Touch

And

Smell

Speech

The same old, the same old, stinking, rotten things.

Time-tested, familiar, limp, lifeless.

Mom, tell me a story.

My raja, which story would you like to hear?

A good one.

Raja! Yes, she always addressed him as Raja. He'd say: How lovely you are . . . lovely.

Mom.

Yes?

A story.

All right, listen.

Son, it rained so hard one day, so mercilessly . . .

Like today?

Yes, son.

What happened then, mom?

She kept wondering what to say next. When the rain came, she began to remember. Then . . .?

Mom.

Yes, my child, listen . . . It was a downpour. The sparrow's nest was made of straw. The crow's was of unbaked mud. The sparrow's house withstood the rain, no worry about the dirt or mud . . .

But, mom, the crow's house was made of mud, which washed away . . .

What? No, son. If it had done so, where would the poor soul go? Whom can he call his own?

Mom, is he still getting soaked in the rain?

No, my raja. He comes to the sparrow's house and tells her . . . to open the door, sister sparrow.

Yes, son.

Did the sparrow open the door?

No.

Why?

Don't know, son, I don't know.

She should open the door. Our teacher tells us to always love our neighbours.

To love one's neighbour, said your teacher.

Your teacher, right?

Yes, why?

No, one cannot love one's neighbour, son.

Why? Is it bad?

No, very good, love . . .

Yes, go on, mom.

She said nothing more; kept caressing her son with affection. And the child kept making little noises. Later on, he fell asleep

Vali Ram Vallabh

with his feet on her belly. She was lost in thought. The light streaked out from the study. She wished he'd go on working all night. She wanted to sleep alone tonight; didn't want to be touched tonight; otherwise her body would speak out. Her body would become the tongue for her soul.

But can everyone follow the tongue of silence?

He could see through it.

He could feel it by a slight touch.

But this? He couldn't comprehend this vernacular.

So what! He has the right. So what if he didn't comprehend the vernacular of silence?

She felt like a prostitute, a helpless poor little thing, dependent, chained down with relationships. She longed to break all bonds, shred them to pieces, to finish them off for ever. She removed her child's feet from her. The child turned on his side and threw his milk-soft arms around her neck. Overcome with love, she stroked the silky hands of her child; tears welled up in her eyes.

Could this web of silk be broken! Never . . .

Perhaps that's why the sparrow had said to the crow.

Wait, I am feeding my child now. . .

He'll grow up, get married, bring his bride; only then will she allow the crow to come in.

Today the web of my child is around my neck.

Tomorrow a grandchild's.

It was the same rain, pouring down without mercy. Thick clouds gathered. He'd come; she'd wiped his hair with the wet corner of her shawl, then they had embraced.

He'd whispered, Now please add a little kohl too . . . such a child I am.

Who is it?' mother had asked.

No one, mother. It is my girlfriend.

All right.

The blind mother kept on counting her beads, sitting in silence.

Both had their tea while it rained, had breakfast.

Both had lent warmth to each other with their embrace.

As the rain relented, he left.

Did she deceive her mother?

Her mother or herself? Or the world?

Perhaps all of the above, but not him.

Really?

She could not go to his house.

His wife stood blocking her way.

Raja, I will have to marry now. Mother won't listen to me anymore.

But we have promised to be each other's, life after life.

True, my Raja, but you are trapped in a relationship.

But, my Rani, that relationship is only outwardly. I am alone.

But it is she who has the right.

How long will you keep on reminding me of that?

She tried and tried, but mother wouldn't listen; finally she said:

I am leaving. Do take care. Protect your falling house.

If I ever showed up at your door, will you let me in?

Of course, you can come any time.

No, you won't be able to do it.

Why not? Why would I not be able to do that? Our youths will pass somehow, but we'll need each other in old age. If we couldn't live together, we could die together at least.

No, I don't want to live that long—tired, bent out of shape, coughing, what will I ask for at your door? What will I be able to give?

Raja, please, don't say such sad things . . . for my sake.

He never came again. Nor did he run into her anywhere. With such restlessness did she pass all those months! Even moments of happiness were spent in a struggle. Now even the memory seemed too old. If he'd showed up then, she would've given everything up to leave with him. If he came now?

This child . . . if he came now, she wouldn't go.

The husband?

Honour?

Society?

She pondered and pondered. She is not alone now. She has children, and people consider her an honourable member of

Vali Ram Vallabh

society; the husband too is not a bad person. The house . . . all this furniture, jewellery, clothes, china, pots and pans . . . no, how can she leave now. So many ties, so many traps.

She kept on thinking. Only God knows when she fell asleep. The light went out in the study. Two feet approached her; and returned after pulling the blanket over the mother and the son. She woke up. Eyes wide open.

She could feel the breeze, heavy breeze. It rained outside.

Oh . . . who's at the door? Who's knocking at the door?

He? He has come? In this rain? Asking for shelter? Asking for help?

He kept waiting all those years?

He was in love all this time? Promise? Memory of touch?

And she? Remained in the trap created by honour, money, children?

Another knock came on the door.

Suddenly she jumped out of her bed. The blanket fell away, leaving the child uncovered.

She reached the door on trembling feet.

He was getting soaked in the rain. He was standing. She would certainly bring him in now.

The world . . . the motherhood . . . will destroy her aloneness.

She placed her hand on the side of the door; she pulled back as though terrified. The corpse of Madame Bovary hung from the door of happiness.

The mistress of Flaubert . . . Madame Bovary.

The lover deceived her.

She swallowed poison. Madame's body writhed. Her body had stiffened because of pain.

The blood had dried on the corners of her lips.

And Madame's husband, madly in love with her.

The little girl, terrified.

Standing at the door of death, Madame Bovary.

She ran to her husband's room.

She threw her arms around his neck, embraced him; how nervous she had become. Poor little Madame Sparrow.

The sparrow's door is shut.
The rain has no intention of letting up.
He is sitting outside.
Alone.
The wretched crow.

—*Translated from the Sindhi by Moazzam Sheikh*

the dying sun

Syed Afzal Haider

Les Ballance, a friend from my college days, arrives in town from Berkeley on a hot Thursday in July, to attend a three-day conference on intestinal disorders. I pick him up from the arrival gate of Continental Airlines. Les dumps his suitcase in the back seat and jumps into the front as we drive off.

'Do not cry over me while I live, or after my death,' says Les, putting on his seat belt.

'What is it?' I ask, 'altitude sickness or a California high?'

'Neither,' he says with a mischievous smile, pushing his glasses up his nose. 'We are all Bodhisattvas of our own selves and we have to keep returning to this material world until we resolve all our issues and have achieved enlightenment.'

'Is that why you've arrived today?' I ask with a smile.

'I am serious,' he says, laughing. 'When all our issues are resolved we attain Nirvana, an internal peace with ourselves.'

'In life, logical thinking is not necessary,' he continues. 'Only the acceptance of "what's happening" or "what has happened" leads one to peace and tranquillity.'

Looking away from the road and turning towards Les, I snap, 'A man without a woman, I can understand, but a child without a mother, I cannot accept.' Looking back at the road again, I say, 'Peace and tranquillity, how dull.'

'Let me tell you about this obese woman,' he says, changing the subject. 'She came to see me with infected intestines. Every time she moved, she exploded like a horse. Even when she was sitting she couldn't control the fireworks.'

'Did Dr Ballance have a cure for her?'

'Some of us are more accepting,' he says, amused with himself. 'Medicine does not have cures for all our ailments. We referred her to Outpatient Psychiatry.'

During my dinner with Les and Marty at Matsuya, Marty looks sad. Nothing works, I think, and I drink too much California Chablis.

'I find life very sad,' says Marty. 'Not so much my own life. I mean life itself is sad.' He takes a sip of wine and continues.

'Everyone I know is dying. My father may die two weeks from now, or several years later, long after I am gone. The fact is we are all dying.'

There is a pause. Marty is getting too serious, I think. There is nothing to say. Besides, I agree. Life is too short to ponder a subject like this. Marty goes on. I take my first big bite of Ika with plenty of wasabi.

'That's why Dylan turned to Jesus,' says Les. 'To be born again . . . and to have something to believe in.'

'I find no need to believe in anything,' says Marty. 'It's the meaninglessness of life that makes me sad.'

I don't know what to say. I have to rush home. I keep wondering about the White Sox. I turn to Marty, my eyes full of tears from too much wasabi and we both start laughing.

When Les and I arrive home, Adam is still up. Dressed in his pyjamas, he is sitting with Sylvia, the baby sitter, at the kitchen table drinking hot chocolate. The TV sitting on the kitchen counter is on, but no one is watching it.

'Sox won,' announces Adam.

'I know,' I say, taking a bottle of St Pauli Girl dark from the refrigerator. I offer one to Les, but he declines. 'I am sorry I don't have any California Coolers,' I say, smiling.

'Never mind,' says Les, sitting beside Adam. 'I don't need to drink to feel better.'

Sylvia smiles and gets up from her chair. 'Let's go to your room,' she says to Adam. 'I'll read you a bedtime story.'

Syed Afzal Haider

Adam looks at me. I nod my head. He gets up from his chair and gives me a kiss.

'Can I get one too?' asks Les.

'No,' says Adam with a smile. He walks over and gives Les a kiss.

'I enjoyed visiting you,' says Les. 'Come and see me in Berkeley. I'll take you to the Golden Gate Bridge.'

Adam says nothing. He walks away holding Sylvia's hand. Stopping at the mid-stair landing, he says, 'Daddy, don't forget to kiss me goodnight before you go to sleep.'

'I won't,' I say, taking a sip of my beer.

'I am with her though she has left me,' says our hero on the tube, in a rerun of a made-for-TV movie.

'You love them and you leave them,' I say. I get up and turn off the TV.

'It's easy for you to say,' says Les. 'You live in self-exile.'

I walk back and sit down beside him. 'You should talk. A new marriage every second child or three years, whichever comes first.'

'I need a woman in my life to feel complete,' says Les. 'Besides, I am not the issue here.'

I take a sip of my beer and say nothing. Les continues. 'It's been four years now since Susanna died, and you live like nothing has happened, like she is going to come back on the next flight.'

It's been only three years, I want to shout. But who is counting?

'Quite the contrary,' I say. 'I live like someone has died and nothing will ever be the same.'

'Yeah, yeah,' says Les, nodding his head. 'I see more pictures of Susanna hanging on the walls now than when she was living.'

You don't need photographs on the walls if the person is living, I want to say, but I am quiet.

Shaking his head, Les says, 'One has to go on living in the face of death.'

'My mother used to say,' I respond, '"To remember me by, to keep my memory alive, you should say your prayers every day, provide for the needy, and be kind to your father.'" I pause and look out of the kitchen window into the dark.

'Except for her child,' I say, 'Susanna left no instructions.'

'It happens every day. Children lose mothers. It just turns out to be your story.'

'Yeah, to you it's a story,' I say sharply.

'Contemplate, but do not question,' says Les in a calm voice. 'Acceptance is the way. You don't need anybody's permission to enjoy life.'

'Now I see why you no longer smoke dope,' I say. 'California living suits you. You are high on life.'

'I'm done preaching,' says Les, getting up. 'Maybe I'll read Adam a bedtime story.' He walks upstairs.

I sit in the kitchen aimlessly reading the morning paper. I hear Sylvia walk downstairs, but I stay busy with yesterday's news. Sylvia says goodbye and leaves.

'Facts about the universe,' Les reads to Adam, sitting next to him in his bed. 'Scientists expect our universe to go on as it has for at least another forty billion years, when all the hydrogen will finally be used up in making new stars. The last star will shine and go out. Our universe will become dark, cold, and lifeless.'

'Are you sad,' asks Adam, 'that one day there will no longer be a sun? No more mornings, no light or heat?'

'Not really,' says Les.

'Why not?' Adam asks.

'Forty billion years is a mighty long time. We'll all be dead by then,' says Les, 'and life will go on in one form or another.'

'I have a shield that'll protect me,' says Adam. 'I am not going to die—never.'

Les kisses him goodnight, and walks to the guest room.

Adam is lying on his bed, looking at pictures in his space book when I walk in. 'Are you sad that one day our sun is going to die?' asks Adam.

'Yes, I am,' I say.

'Will you be dead then?' he asks.

Syed Afzal Haider

'Yeah,' I say absently.

'I'll protect you,' he says. 'I have a shield.'

'That will be nice,' I say, sitting down on his bed.

'Les has read me a story,' he says. 'Will you lie down with me and just tell me a short story?' he asks.

'Yes,' I say, lying down beside him.

'Once there was a magnificent king and his vivacious queen,' I begin. 'They lived happily, and they grew old together. And one morning they both did not wake up from their sleep,' I say. 'And that's the end of the story.'

'That was the shortest story I've ever heard,' he says. 'Tell me another.'

'I'll tell you my favourite story,' I say. I can't remember who told me this story or what makes it my favourite. 'There once was a kind farmer,' I start.

'His name was Krishna. One year from spring to fall there was no rain, not even a single wandering drop. It was the worst drought ever. All of Krishna's land dried up like a potter's fired pots. He had no money. His wife Seeta couldn't bear him a child, and his elderly parents were losing their sight.'

'What does losing sight mean?' asks Adam.

'Not being able to see,' I say. 'With the passage of time.'

'Am I going to be blind?' he asks.

'No.'

'How can you tell?'

'It's hereditary. Like the chances of getting bald,' I say.

'I won't mind being bald,' he says, shaking his head. 'I want to be able to see my mommy.'

'I want to see her, too,' I say.

'I just want to see if she is 'kay 'kay,' he says.

The wind rustles against the skylight.

'Are all dead people 'kay, 'kay?' he asks.

'I would like to think so,' I say. 'We have to live with what we've got,' I say.

'Yeah, and with what we don't got,' says Adam.

'We can miss her,' I say quietly.

'And we can be sad about it,' says Adam.

'It passes,' I say.

'What about Krishna?' asks Adam.

'One day, a black witch appeared and knocked on his door. "You have been a kind person," said the black witch to Krishna when he opened the door. 'I shall grant you one wish."'

'Only one wish?' asks Adam, sounding disappointed.

'Yes,' I say.

'So what did Krishna ask for?'

'Krishna wished that his parents could see his son eat on plates made of gold.'

'That was clever,' says Adam.

'Yeah,' I say, smiling. 'Krishna was a wise man.'

I lie in Adam's bed until he falls asleep. I kiss him on the forehead before retiring to my room.

I dream that Ringo Starr dies from drinking too many wine coolers. Ringo's body, dressed in a pink tuxedo, is lying in an open coffin on a stage. The band is playing. Pete Best is on the drums. John and Paul are singing 'In My Life' for a farewell concert at Ringo's funeral when George walks on to the stage. There is a loud applause that wakes me up. I want to close my eyes and listen to the music. I want to hear the Beatles sing 'Long and Winding Road'. I hear Adam cry. I get out of my bed and walk to Adam's room and ask him what is wrong.

'I don't want to dream anymore,' says Adam with his eyes closed.

'What are you dreaming about?' I ask.

'About you,' he says, turning to his side.

'What about me?' I ask.

There is no answer. Adam is asleep again. I sit down on his bed. In a dim yellow light filtering through the skylight, I see the titles of the books sitting on the bookshelf. Stuffed among his books is a model kit for a 1932 Ford 'Victoria'. I reach out and pick it up. I hold the unopened, cellophane-wrapped box in my

Syed Afzal Haider

hand for a moment, wondering if I should spend the late hours of the night putting 'Vicky' together. I laugh at the thought and put the box back on the shelf.

I hear Adam talk in his sleep. Just like Susanna used to do, he kicks his covers off. I get up, cover him, and walk out of his room.

I lie down on my bed until the grey dawn arrives. With my eyes wide open, I think of different endings to my story, using the same beginning, same middle, and the same sequence of events, but I can't figure out how to connect the happenings with the end, or the end with the beginning. I think of getting up, taking a long shower, and saying Fajr prayers like my mother used to do every morning, but then decide against it. I don't want to shock the soul of my deceased mother.

I drive Les to the airport. Adam comes along for the ride. Sitting in the back seat, Adam asks Les, 'Are you sad that you're leaving?'

'I am going to miss you,' Les replies.

I think Les didn't answer the question.

On the way back from the airport, Adam says he is sad. He cries most of the way back.

'When I was a little boy,' I say, trying to comfort him, 'every time someone left, I thought I'd never see that person again. I still feel that way, but I know better.'

'But you saw them again,' says Adam.

'Yeah,' I say, looking at the setting sun.

'Why did you feel that way?'

'I don't know,' I say. 'Feelings are hard to explain. Besides, there are very few explanations to our "whys".'

'I know,' he says quietly, looking away. The pale yellow sun is setting. 'I am sad that the sun is going to die one day,' he says.

'Yeah,' I say absently. 'The thought of having no sun does bother me.'

jungle

Ikramullah

The sun had set and everywhere the greyness had deepened when a bus came to a halt near a thicket of trees. He got off the bus wearing a starched salwar made of lattha fabric, almost rustling. The conductor yelled, 'Move on!' The bus sped off with a screech. A strip of light that emerged from the door to cast itself upon the street now ran along with the bus. He kept his eyes glued to the back of the bus, where a black steel ladder went up to the roof. He could see through the back window his fellow passengers' heads, partially hidden behind the soiled, unwashed turbans and warm shawls with faded colours. They all looked straight ahead and bobbed in their seats. He stood alone by the roadside; the bus had vanished from his sight. A bit of dust and a little smoke lingered in the air. His gaze met with the dark fields stretched far into the distance. Behind them, waited a jungle, arms extended from one edge of the sky to the other. In the haze, the jungle looked like a dark wall reaching to the sky. Except for the birds hurrying towards the jungle, the entire landscape appeared to be a frozen painting. He took a piss by the side of a tree and then slung a sack across his shoulders, containing the physical manifestation of his feelings for his parents and his wife-to-be. Walking down the slope by the side of the street, he pulled himself on a narrow path. He would reach the jungle in an hour; then, after walking through the breadth of the

Originally published as 'Jungle' in *Jungle*, Sang-e Meel Publishers, 1990, Lahore jungle for two hours, he would emerge to find his village right there at the end.

Dogs began to bark. From the darkness the shapes of tiny houses suddenly began to materialize before him—Had he already reached his village? — He didn't have to walk through the jungle? —Rows of closed doors stood deaf and mute on each side of the deserted street. Forlornness seemed to rain down everywhere. He walked ahead, utterly confused. His feet sank in the lifeless dust on the street. Wherever his feet touched it, the dust would rise to chase them and remain hanging in the air. Anyone of these unfriendly doors could very well be the door of his home; perhaps he should just knock on one! A shop was open at the village's main square. Inside, a shadow was seen sitting in the flickering glow of an earthen lamp. It seemed as though it had been sitting there, bowed head, silently, for centuries. Was it alive or a mere corpse? Nothing could be said for certain from this distance. I should take a peek, he thought, to check if the figure was alive or dead. But he moved ahead, thinking, 'If it is alive, it will die eventually, and if it is already dead, then, what can I do?' As he approached the last house in the village, he saw a person wrapped inside a white blanket headed his way. As he walked past the man, he heard a voice.

Stranger! O stranger! His feet came to a halt. He turned and waited. About ten yards from him the man also stood facing him.

'Do you wish to speak to me?'

'Yes, where are you going?'

'Across the jungle.'

'A stranger won't be able to find his way through it even in daylight, and you want to try it at night!'

'I am not a stranger; I have known every leaf of this jungle since childhood.'

'Look, this is the last village before the jungle. There is no other village in your path where you could break your journey. Stay the night here and come morning, go on to your destination.'

'No, you don't need to worry. Tonight the moon should be out in a short while. I won't have any trouble finding my way.'

'This is a very dangerous jungle.'

'Not for me though; I know it inside out,' and saying that, he walked away.

'Don't be stubborn; listen to my advice.'

Ignoring the advice, he kept on trudging ahead on the zigzagging path between the fields. The other man, the white blanket wrapped about him, watched him walking away. (He wished to call the stranger back one last time before he vanished from his sight, but he could not summon the courage to do it.)

The stranger stood below this unusually long wall. The narrow path entered the jungle like a snake enters its hole. He stopped as he arrived there. Due to extreme proximity, this unusually long wall was only visible for a few yards to the right and to the left. The branches atop the thick trunks of these absolutely dark trees intricately intertwined with each other. The clouds made up of dark leaves seemed on the verge of rain. How many changes, he wondered, must have taken place in the period of three years! It is better perhaps that I turn back to the last village. He tested the hard earth on the path with his foot; his feet were restive like a strong horse. The old sensations associated with this path revisited him. This *is* the same old path; I recognize it so well! The path that enters the jungle here entered the jungle at the same point previously as well and left the jungle, in a straight line, at the other side. So far I haven't detected any change. Well, let's drop this business of whether a change has occurred or not, no sense in risking my neck for nothing. The thing that carried me across the jungle at night was my sixth sense. Let's see if my sixth sense is awakened or not by entering it. I won't go too deep, just a short incursion. He lowered the duffel from his shoulder to hold it in one hand and, brushing aside the branches with the other, he stepped into the jungle. He took a deep breath: it was the same old, subdued fragrance and the moist, heavy air. Outside was dark too, yet one could still distinguish between the tall crops and the flat ground under the starlight. Bushes resembled dogs crouching stiffly on their behinds. The outlines of the trees'

Ikramullah

dark umbrellas could also be made out. But inside it was so dark that one could not find even one's own hand. He looked up and around to check if he could spot a star, but no, nothing, just darkness after darkness; a boundless obscurity stretched itself far and beyond. Still looking up in search of a star, he took a few more steps, 'Yes, there it is!' A lone star twinkled deep in the sky. With intervals, its light expanded and shrank in such a way that one thought it were a heart beating silently in the distance. Where have its other mates disappeared? Why, where else could they be if not behind the leaves. Let's search for more stars. His face up as before, he stepped forward. With his first step he lost the star. He kept on moving ahead. In a space between the rising peaks of the trees two stars trembled, riveted close to each other. How my sixth sense has guided me to this place so far! I've walked precisely on the narrow path. My feet have not forgotten these paths. I can reach my village soon, so what's the point of turning back to the village I left behind. How much distance have I covered so far? One furlong, perhaps! A little less or a little more is possible too; a furlong and a quarter or even a half, it's difficult to say. There is a burr tree somewhere here at about the same distance, which is really gigantic. It is about forty paces from the path, to the right. There is no bigger tree than this in the entire jungle. In the days of my youth I used to venture this far with friends picking wood and then in daylight we would play hide and seek in its dense branches. What a strong and compact tree it was, standing with its feet planted firmly in the earth's chest resembling a mountain of respectability. I wonder if it is still there or not? I should see it. It is still evening, not that late at all. He pressed the path with his feet so they would hold on to its memory. He then turned right, joined his heels, and stood at attention. He took a good measure of body and, breathing deeply, began to walk in the direction of his nose as is done when measuring a piece of land. He stretched forward his right arm and, counting his steps, set out in search of the burr tree. He had hardly gone six, seven steps when his hand came into contact with a tree. Running his hand over its rough bark, then circling it, cautiously taking one step at a time and managing to avoid collisions with trees, he took another fifty steps. The great tree still had not been found. As he moved farther away from the narrow path, the woods became denser. His right hand that moved before him now bumped into trees frequently. Despite care, his left shoulder would ram into a tree, and he would feel as though someone had grabbed his shoulder on purpose and pushed him cruelly. There never used to be any trees around the burr tree! It dominated a small patch of earth all by itself. The ropes dangling from its thick branches swayed in the air, and many of them had penetrated the earth and now supported the tree's heavy arms-like pillars. We used to call that the tree's beard. So as not to be caught by a playmate, who was chasing us, we would climb up and down through the beard. If I am walking in the right direction, I should have reached the tree by now. That means I took the right turn from the narrow path a little too soon. So if I turn left now and walk parallel to the path, it is possible to find the tree. I will search for it for some distance, then return to the path, and from there head straight to my village. He changed his direction. 'Well, the path runs in a straight line, doesn't it? Whenever I want, I can turn to the path by simply turning left and, counting sixty paces, I will be back on it.' He was walking when he kicked something and, in a state of helplessness, he came down to the muddy ground. His sack rolled off and away. 'The hand stretched before me did not see it coming. The slippery mud arrived too soon, and I slipped on it. No, I kicked something!' He searched the ground with both hands and discovered a clean and flat stump of a tree as big as that of a butcher's to cut the meat on. Bent to his side like a weaver ready to thread the loom, he dragged himself a few feet to look for his sack, veering to the right in the mud, and then to the left. Taking one step forward again, he turned right first, then left, but did not find his sack. He took one more step in that weaver's stance. Then a few more and his hand struck the sack covered with

Ikramullah

mud. His hand had grazed against many tree stumps while searching for his sack. Ah, so many trees have been chopped down in this part of the jungle! They must have watered the area too. He looked up. A vast patch of dark sky studded with stars revealed itself to him. This seems like a decent-sized field! 'After walking through the trees beyond the field, I will certainly find the burr tree. But I am finding walking impossible. Why am I making a big deal out of this tree? I wasted my time for nothing. I would have wrapped up half of my journey by now.' Returning to the trees once again, facing the narrow path, he retraced and counted his steps. Having gone fifty paces, he tapped the earth with his feet. It was the usual soft earth, where the occasional blades of grass whispered to his trousers. Now he took every step with extreme care, verifying the ground beneath his feet before the next step. He completed sixty steps in this way in the hope of finding the path. But, no, this was not it. To further remove doubt from his mind he checked the earth with his hands. Perhaps it had fooled my feet! It was the same earth that belonged to the jungle and the same long blades of grass entering his nostrils. 'The way I had walked sixty steps away from it I have walked back as well with utmost care. Where on earth did the narrow path go? I may have perhaps taken a longer route coming back, so I should go a few more yards and see.' No, there was no trace of it. He walked back; then walked again; then walked back again. He tried walking in circles, but to no avail. Exasperated, he began to reflect, 'Why did I leave it? More importantly, why did I enter the jungle in the first place? I would have been sound asleep in the last village at the moment. Anyway, where could the path go after all? And I have not really ventured too deep in the jungle by any means, hardly two furlongs. This is quite close to the edge. Even if I do not find the path, I could weave myself through the trees to get out.' His shoes felt heavy. He found a dry piece of wood to clean the mud off the soles of his shoes. He then decided to remove the mud from his clothes and sack, but declined to pursue it because of the tedious nature of the job. Let it be. In order to take a little rest he leaned against the sack. He dozed off. He did not know how long he was asleep. He woke up when a pack of jackals turned the jungle upside down with their howls. 'Oh, jackals!' A soft smile covered his face involuntarily. 'What else is there in this jungle except for these jackals!' The moonlight had disseminated itself over the trees. The sweet light filtered down through the leaves. Observing the moonlight, he experienced a sweet feeling of surprise, joy, and sense of calm. It had completely escaped his mind in the hustle that the moon had to come out at night. Right in front of him shone the grassless narrow path like a snake with a spotted skin. '*Why*! I must have crossed it at least twenty times. I am surprised I could not tell; this is the very path I had been going insane looking for. How did my feet forget the memory of its touch? How could they lose their sense of memory?'

The sack slung over his shoulder, he turned back to go to the last village. 'I will crash there for now and renew my journey tomorrow at sunrise. That man wrapped in the white blanket who insisted that I stay must now be comfortably asleep in his home. How am I going to knock on every closed door of the village and ask about the man in the white blanket whom I had met at the end of the village! God knows how many men must have walked to the end of the village that evening wrapped inside a white blanket! I don't even remember his face. But how could I? Half hidden, his face was a plain slate of darkness. Besides, how can one knock on hundreds of doors. Well, then, I will stay at the mosque. But the muezzin must have locked up the mosque, which he will open in the morning only. What good will it do me then? My clothes are wet and it is getting colder. I haven't eaten anything since morning. Hunger has lit a fire in my stomach. Too many needs to be taken care of. Who is going to satisfy them there! If no one opens the door, then, if nothing else, the village dogs will keep barking at me. So should I turn back to my village? No, no, the residents of this village cannot be so cold-hearted that they won't give shelter to a traveller at night.

Ikramullah

But if the owner of the house, where I will spend the night, murdered me for the five hundred rupees, which I have saved up bit by bit in the last three years, and buried me in his house, no one is ever going to find out. Then I will have to wash my hands off my life and money both. *Oh-ho*, so that is the cause of my reluctance. It took me this long to scratch and see the real thing that sat hiding in my heart like a thief.' He stopped. He turned and saw the flat, plain narrow path leading straight afar like a snake with a spotted skin. 'Just like that it comes out at the other side of the jungle. It is impossible for it to disappear in the moonlight. Even if the moonlight were not there, there is little chance that I will lose sight of it. The two or two and a half feet wide, hard and compact earth where shoes produce solid noise is completely different from the soft and slippery earth of the jungle. The reason my feet had earlier failed to find the path was either because I must have jumped over it or when I slowly felt the earth with my extended foot, I could not feel the difference because of the mud sticking to the soles of my shoes. In fact, I should have tested the earth by hitting my heels hard. I would have found it out right away. Well, that was a mistake! Man learns with experience. This time I dare not step off the path. The stupidity and foolishness I committed when I decided to go in search of the burr tree can only be due to my ignorance and lack of common sense. Especially since I have gone through so much trouble I am not likely to repeat the mistake.' Once again he turned towards his village. Setting the sack on his shoulder, he hurried on the dotted path. Soon, on the right side of the path, he reached the point where trees had been chopped down. It was an oval-shaped open field. The moon shone spryly above the field's right shoulder. To his left the branches of the trees, which travelled along the path, hung down like lifeless limbs. The tree stumps the butchers use were strewn everywhere, shining helplessly. The morning haze had begun to spread itself now across the dark sky. So many stars, which until recently glowed brightly, now vanished behind the effulgent mist. Only a few stars, scattered here and there, could still be seen as though they had faded. Once again the jungle had grown from both sides. As he covered a little more distance, he noticed, behind the trees, apart from anything else, more prominent than others, the huge, dark dome bathing in the moonlight. 'Ah, so here it is!' He stared at the burr tree with disgust, spat on the ground, and, keeping a straight face, remained on his path. An unclear, ambiguous thought, which had been floating in the back of his head for quite some time, now formed itself in a tangibly concrete shape. 'Where on earth am I rushing? What is there? What would have happened if I had reached there by now? And what if I never reach there, then what? Nothing! It is the same thing as the situation with the burr tree. That when I was going mad looking for it, what would have happened if I had found it? And now that I have found it on my way, what difference did it really make? A little disgust and that is all. I could have expressed happiness as well and that would have been it. Perhaps, I would have felt its rough bark, but what difference would even that have made! Still, I would have not succeeded in touching its essence.'

In the meanwhile he had crossed half of the jungle and the moonlight had vanished as if someone had turned off the switch. A patch of cloud obscured the moon, but a little bit of brightness still managed to sneak out through one edge of the cloud. The same branches, which had seemed lifeless just a while back, now seemed as though countless snakes hung from the tree, writhing tortuously. A restless and swift breeze moved noisily, whistling, rustling through the leaves. The trees, time and again, were banging their heads against each other. Since he was in the thick of the jungle, he was not directly in the way of the breeze, still his clothes fluttered constantly. Where did the clouds and the breeze come from suddenly? 'The breeze must have picked up gradually, and I could not realize, as I was lost in my thoughts. Had I diverted my thought towards the breeze, would I have been able to stop the storm? Or stop the cloud from covering the moon?' Just as he was watching, the very last ray of light

Ikramullah

disappeared. Complete darkness took over all around him. 'Should I return to the previous village? But that would be the same distance as my village. He struck the path with his heel carefully; it had not disappeared from under his feet. I should go as far as I can, and if I get lost, I will lean against a tree, spend the night there and find my way home in the morning.' Though he slowed his pace, he kept walking. Every fifteen, twenty steps he would strike his heel against the ground to assure himself that he had not gone astray. It was still underneath him. As he walked deep into the jungle, all of him seemed to have collided with a wall suddenly, injuring his mouth, nose, forehead, neck, chest, belly, legs, everything. Under a spell of dizziness, he fell down, half unconscious; it seemed as though he had collapsed in the ring after not being able to take the continuous punches from a strong opponent. He remained there for a few short moments, trying to gather his senses. Finally he propped himself up slightly on his right elbow. He looked around and encountered absolute darkness. The moon had vanished, the stars had vanished, the sky had vanished; the earth was there still. Still and solid! He felt the ground around him with his hand. He was sitting on the narrow path. 'Is it that someone has built right on the path here? They must have chopped down dry branches and logs from shisham and kikar trees into smaller pieces and stacked them up in piles. That must be what I smacked myself into. He ran his hand over his face and it felt wet. 'Blood—no, must be sweat'; his entire body was covered with a light sweat. His eyes widening as much as possible, he tried to examine his hand at close range. He could not tell whether it was blood or sweat in the dark. A taste of saltiness formed in his mouth. But sweat too is salty. But now his tongue felt the taste of blood undoubtedly. Puckering his lips, he tried to gather as much blood as possible in one go and spat it out on the ground. For an instant, he felt his mouth clean. Yet the next moment the taste of blood re-emerged on his tongue. The entire face hurt. The eyes hurt too, still he could not comprehend how many places he had been injured, and how severe the injury was. 'Perhaps I had hurt my eyes too. Just as when I press other parts of my body and in turn feel a lazy and sluggish pain, I experience the same pain when I press my eyes. Woods are not supposed to be gathered right on the path! It has to be kept clear. So, then, is it not that narrow path? Perhaps the labourers who collect wood in the jungle have given it the shape of a path by constantly walking on it.'

'Having strayed from the real path, I have been walking on this one, God knows since when. This too is hard and compact like the other one, and my heels have tried their best to assure me of that; my heels were not capable of doing anything more. Now, am I facing the stack of woods or is it facing my back? He began crawling on all fours. He would wave his arm in the air before him to see if there was anything in his way, then crawl forward, spitting blood from time to time. 'What? What is this? One narrow path, and another one crossing over it? I am at the crossroads! Is the other path the one I had walked on? Or is it this one?' In search of his cloth sack, he crawled down from the narrow path like a four-legged animal to the soft earth and dry grass of the jungle. His hand felt the rise of another path. 'Which path is mine among these? Could it be the case where the same path is moving ahead in a circular way and my hands and knees are coming upon it again and again and all this time I have been taking it to be more than one? Now another one! No, this cannot be just one path. These are separate.' He forgot about the sack and crawled faster. Another path—then another one—and yet another—what is going on? There was a time when finding just one was impossible; now there is no stopping them. He banged his head against something. He felt the hurdle with his hand. It was a stack of wood gathered in the jungle. He stood up. 'Is it the previous stack or a new one? There does not seem to be any difference between them. These were the walls made of the same kind of twisted, uneven sticks of wood. If indeed it were a different pile, did it lie on the right side of the earlier pile or left? It is quite possible it was right behind it, or even before it; there could

Ikramullah

be as many stacks as paths. What direction did I take to arrive here? Perhaps from right.' He turned that way. His body was trembling, his face and clothes were soaked with blood. He was out of breath. After taking a few steps, he considered, 'No, I must have come from the other direction. He turned around. No, no, I came from the left side.' Suddenly he changed his direction again. His head bumped into a branch dangling downwards. The sound of a loud thud echoed in his head. Recovering from the blow, the first question his mind posed: 'Where on earth have I been trapped? The jungle has laid siege to me.' The sound of its laughter pierced his ears. 'It won't let me be. I must run away from here.' He took off in the direction of his nose. The way he bobbed up and down after colliding with trees suggested the players were kicking the soccer ball to each other standing in a circle, but were not allowing it to fall outside the ring. At last, he dropped to the ground. In the morning when the sun came out ants had already covered his body from head to toe. It was impossible to discern who had been killed in the dark of night.

—*Translated from the Urdu by Moazzam Sheikh*

feeqa's death

Nadir Ali

I dreamed of Feeqa today after so many years . . . The message a dream brings is unique and complex each time. Feeqa's case, however, is different. I had erased both his life and death from my memory. But he borrowed a new mask this time.

A water-carrier all his life, he sat today as Husaina Mehr's helper at the fruit shop. I picked up a melon and held it out to him in the dream. But Feeqa spoke, 'Little master, you didn't pick up the melon from this shop, so I can't take any money for this. Enjoy!' Laughing, he turned to Husaina Mehr, 'You haven't kept melons here, Mehr. It must belong to another shop,' and then he said to me, 'You are mistaken, boss,' and laughed. Husaina peered inside the shop and found no melons there. The dream ended. I woke up happy with a free melon.

Dreams are strange enactments of life's song and dance. Even if we pick apart each strand of the rope, we won't understand them. This is the mistake psychologists make. They'd say it is the mother symbol or the sex symbol. But both these thrusts are wrong . . . Each strand is a different song and when you knit these strands into the rope of life, each twist then manifests a different dance! The thing was that Feeqa had stolen a melon for me once from Husaina's field, which was situated behind the shops. From that point on we were always on the prowl to steal

Originally published as 'Feeqe di Moat' in *Kahani Lekha*, Rut Lekha Publishers, 2001, Lahore melons at night. So Feeqa had reminded me, today, of a favour from the forgotten past by giving me the stolen melon . . . But there was another twist to it too . . . Feeqa had committed a murder which only Husaina Mehr and I had witnessed.

Swai Ram's shop was next to Mehr's. At dawn, the thoroughfare was completely empty. It was time for the cart delivering ice blocks to show up. Husaina Mehr unloaded fruit boxes inside to stack them up. He had had a quarrel with Sheeda the ice-vendor the morning before which Feeqa and I had seen. I had taken our cows to the City Park, where grazing was prohibited, and was headed back at the first hint of morning. At that time, Sheeda was unloading the ice blocks and piling them up on the platform of Swai Ram's shop. Sheeda was on dope, had an ugly mug, and enjoyed cussing with his pig-like face. Mehr was a simple man and didn't like messing with anyone. 'O, Mehr, let me shove this little mango up your ass!' This was enough to invite trouble. Mehr grabbed a piece of brick from the shop and hurled it at Sheeda. It hit him on the forehead. Feeqa and I rushed, pushing the two away from each other . . . 'Let me go and unload the ice, and if I don't return to shove a bamboo up your ass, Mehr, I ain't my father's son.'

'Son, you don't seem to be one anyway,' Mehr dared him.

Early next morning Mehr and Sheeda were grabbing each other. Feeqa stood in the midst disentangling them even before I arrived. Sheeda's eyes were bloodshot and his temper was high. He was a habitual criminal and Mehr always tried to restrain him. Those were the Partition days; besides Sheeda had his eyes on Swai Ram. He even said to Feeqa a few times, 'Shouldn't we take off the bloody Hindu's dhoti?' On a few occasions he didn't pay for the soda bottles and had also demanded twice as much for the ice delivery the last time. Scared, Swai Ram dished out the money, but complained to Mehr. The friendship between Mehr and Swai Ram was deep and time-tested.

We used to listen to the news on Swai Ram's radio, and the songs as well. Swai Ram would read the news aloud from

'Parbhaat' every day. Most people in the square were illiterates like Feeqa and Mehr. Swai Ram was an educated and political person. The faces of Mahatma Gandhi and the Muslim Frontier Gandhi had been painted on each side of the 'Royal Soda Water Factory' signboard 'by Sarwar Painter'. Most of us, including the painter, did not even know who the other Gandhi was.

While painting, Sarwar Painter gradually became a Muslim League leader, and while listening to the songs and reading the newspaper, I too became a neighbourhood leader. See, how I have digressed . . . the digressing thread, however, has a connection not only with the murder Feeqa committed but with his death as well.

Later I learned from Feeqa that Sheeda had cursed and challenged the moment he arrived. The whole thing got out of control and he started harassing Mehr. Mehr and Sheeda were exchanging blows; Feeqa too got embroiled in it though his intent actually was to pry them away from each other.

I arrived at the scene soon after and immediately attempted to disengage them. Suddenly, Sheeda's hand reached for the cart. The ice pick was in his grip. 'Sheeda's holding the ice pick, Feeqa!' I cried in alarm.

Mehr was an older man and heavyset, but Feeqa was simply lightning made flesh. He twisted Sheeda's wrist and, grabbing the pick, stabbed him three times in the chest. The blood left its splashes on Feeqa's and Mehr's clothes. Blood poured out of Sheeda's nose as well and he fell back, writhing. He raised his hand in the air once, then went cold.

'What the hell has happened, Mehr? He's dead.'

Though I was the youngest, I hadn't become the neighbourhood leader for nothing. 'Run, you two. No one has seen it.'

Feeqa was shit scared. It had all happened in a flash solely because of his speed. Come to think of it, he had not quarrelled with Sheeda. But he was a loyal friend, and his friendship was deep with Mehr. He used to sprinkle water in front of everyone's shops, including Mehr's. He filled their pitchers as well, but of

Nadir Ali

late there was not much demand for a water-carrier. Mehr always helped out and looked after him.

Well, what had to come to pass had already happened. Mehr and Feeqa both ran off. I felt unusually brave standing at a distance. There was no one around. The first few horse-drawn carriages were about to arrive . . . The early morning walkers were usually Hindus; however, they rarely came out of their houses for walks in the terrifying summer of 1947.

I tethered the cows. As I looked out from the rooftop, I spotted a tongawalla shouting aloud, 'Murder, there has been a murder!' Mehr sauntered out of his house slowly and mingled with the crowd. Feeqa too had filled his water sack again and, after a fleeting glance, began sprinkling the street as though nothing had happened. I was impatient to reach the place of action and, telling Mother about the commotion at the corner, rushed over to the spot to take a second look at Sheeda. His eyes were wide open and the open flaps of his dhoti had left him denuded in the front. Dhurrey Shah the tongawalla, who was the big bad boy of the neighbourhood, covered the front and said, 'Someone's finished him off. Mehr, go and break the news to his family. We'll catch the murderer, rest assured. What motherfucker would've dared to do this in our neighbourhood? Sheeda's murderer must be from some village. I know them well. Dhurrey Shah is still alive.' He went on with his sermon.

Feeqa, Mehr, and I communicated to each other through our eyes. Feeqa had become further disoriented when I saw him in the evening. I tried to calm him down, 'I haven't told anyone, and Mehr is not going to either. No one suspects you.'

The police carried out a cursory investigation. Blood was cheap in those days for murders had become an everyday affair. The knowledge of this secret made me feel like a big boy. 'Feeqa, I haven't even told Mother.'

'Tell her if you want the entire neighbourhood to know,' Feeqa laughed. Mehr had always been a man of few words. Swai Ram felt safer now, after Sheeda's death.

Finally, Swai Ram was the sole casualty of our area in 1947. Dhurrey Shah had been breaking locks on the morning of 15 August . . . Among the Hindu shops, Swai Ram's was the only one open. He decided to lock it up. Dhurrey Shah was drunk. He came up and stabbed Swai Ram. This was the second murder I had seen within a week.

The whole world changed. I became a member of the National Volunteer Corps. Feeqa became loquacious. He would sing all night long. Walking around, he'd beat the rhythm on his water sack, 'akhiyan mila ke, jiya bharma ke, challe nahin jana!' Yet he had changed somehow. Mehr told me six months later that he had taken to drinking rotgut. The affliction finished him off within a year. I moved from the city to Lahore and then I became a government officer. While on vacation, I'd visit Mehr to buy fruit. His mention of Feeqa would bring tears to my eyes, 'Boss, a good man's life is tough.' Mehr was a good man too; he left the world quickly. Feeqa faded from my memory. Last night, he gave me the melon—an excuse to remember me, and be remembered.

—*Translated from the Punjabi by Moazzam Sheikh*

Nadir Ali

a letter from india

Intizar Husain

Precious as my own mortality, may you be blessed, dearest one, with obedience, success and accomplishment; may you live a long life whose courtyard is beautified with posterity and prosperity! After expressing words of blessing and a strong desire to see you again, I would like to mention that we have spent this period of time with no news of your welfare, in a state of misery. I have tried, in several ways, to send you word of our well-being and receive a line from you regarding yours, but my efforts have borne no fruit. I also sent a letter to Ibrahim's son, Yousaf, instructing him to have it forwarded to the prescribed destination in Karachi, and to send me the reply that he would receive from Karachi. As you might have heard through the grapevine, he is employed in Kuwait receiving a handsome salary. But it has gone to his head, as he felt himself bound by no sense of obligation whatsoever to make known to me whether he ever sent you the letter or not, and whether he received one from you or not. Later Sheikh Sadeeq Hassan Khan's son was on his way to London, and I handed him a letter as well, addressed to Karachi, for him to enclose in an envelope and drop in a letterbox in London. That sink of iniquity, too, has not bothered to put my mind at ease by letting me know whether he ever fulfilled his promise or whether his promise will outlive me.

Originally published as 'Hindustan Se Ek Khat' in *Kacchve*, Sang-e Meel Publishers, 1989, Lahore

Imran mian has been the source of the greatest apprehension, for we still do not know if he has reached there or not, and if he did indeed reach there, then he should have sent us word regarding his safety. This is how the events unfolded: Imran mian happened to be passing by here about two months after the war. Since it was early winter, I had moved my bed from my room to the big living room. One night, we heard a knock on the door, and I was worried, God protect us, for who could have showed up at this odd hour? Carefully, I opened the door, surveyed the person who had knocked at the door, and I was struck with surprise and worry. Blood recognized blood—if not for that, there is nothing left to recognize anything, anywhere. Then I embraced him and said, Child, we did not send you off to Pakistan looking like this. What have you done to yourself? But then I felt ashamed at my words, for I should have been grateful that our entrusted one had returned, for you must be thankful to Allah the Merciful and never allow a word of complaint on the tongue lest it becomes that of an infidel's declaration and the proclaimer of it deserving of punishment. Man, stricken with the vice of speech, committed all sorts of follies upon coming into this world, and what with all the other kinds of foolishness he has exhibited since then, has not much room to complain. He should just close his lips and fear the Subduer and the Compeller.

Your chachi was stunned when she recognized Imran mian; then she embraced him and wept her heart out. Though I was careful to be silent, she could not resist asking, 'Where is our daughter-in law? Where have you left the children?' Hearing that, Imran mian suddenly looked ill. Your chachi and I grew worried, and then took great care to make no mention of it during our conversation.

Imran mian stayed here for three days, but what a stay! There was no talking, no laughing. Dazed, Imran mian proposed on the third day that we go to dear Father's grave. I patted his head with affection, and then said, 'Son, you would be reciting fateha on your grandfather's grave after twenty-five years, but

Intizar Husain

circumstances demand that you not go in that direction during the day. You were born on this very soil, and you would surely be recognized there.' He smiled bitterly at that and said, 'Chacha jan, I have already wandered about the town before coming home; the soil did not recognize me.' I said to him, 'Child, it is perhaps better that the soil does not recognize you now.' Be that as it may, come evening, I took Imran mian to the graveyard. I showed him the recent graves; the older ones he recognized himself, though because of the darkness it was hard to find some of them at first. Imran mian's eyes seemed on the verge of tears; mine were moist too. Father jani's grave has grown quite run down, and the haar-singhaar tree that stood by the gravestone embraced the dust some time back. You might still remember how beloved Father was so fond of haar-singhaar trees, and had planted many of them in the garden with fondness, and the trees bore flowers in such abundance that the dupattas of all the girls of the house were dyed with them all year round, and they were added to the biryani dish cooked every time guests came to dinner, and still we would be left with more of them. But haar-singhaars need tending, and how long and how much can I attend to everything by myself? The lone haar-singhaar tree that had stood shading father jani's grave was struck down in the monsoon before the war. Now our garden, and the graveyard too, are without the haar-singhaar tree. Only God's name is for ever! The poor garden is still with us, and that is something at least; only because it was next to the graveyard, they considered it an extension of the graveyard, and we just about managed to hold on to it. So many trees have come down in the last twenty-seven years, and so many memories have been buried along with them that one should perhaps consider the garden a graveyard as well. The ones which still defy their perhaps inevitable fall seem like the gravestones of the days gone by. Anyway, Imran mian has seen the condition the garden is in now as it breathes its last; if he has arrived there, then he must have recounted it to you. He said his farewell the same morning. He passed the entire night sitting by the graves, and so did I. Only when dawn broke, and the sparrows chirped, did he stand up, shaking himself awake, and make a request to leave. Wondering why he was leaving, I asked, 'Now that you have returned, you might as well stay,' to which he then responded dejectedly, 'But no one even recognizes me here.' So I said, 'It is more appropriate that one is not recognized.' But he was not convinced by what I had said, as he was possessed by the idea of travelling. I asked, 'Son, but where will you go?'

'Wherever my feet will take me,' he answered. I gathered that he would try to sneak out to Kathmandu, and from there work out a way to reach Karachi. His decision lay heavy on our hearts, but I decided to endure the separation, partly because of his insistence and partly because I was afraid the news would eventually leak out. Untying it from around my arm, I tied the noor-prayer amulet around his arm with my own hands and gave him into God's care and protection. Parting, I strictly advised him to send us word of his safety by any means possible as soon as he crossed the border. But an eternity has passed and there has been no news of him.

The news from your side of the border trickles in, and it is not what one's heart likes to believe. One day Sheikh Sadeeq Hassan came over to share a piece of news with us, that everybody in Pakistan had become a socialist and onions were selling at five rupees a seer. My heart sank hearing that, but then I thought that Sheikh saheb is a Congressy and any news he would offer concerning Pakistan would be of this nature. One cannot trust him. Within a few days we received news, which took care of the mean-spirited propaganda, that the mirzais had been declared non-Muslims in Pakistan. Sheikh saheb grew long-faced when I broke the news to him. May God keep Pakistan under His blessing and reward the nation for treading the virtuous path; as far as our story is concerned, well, saheb, we live in an Infidelistan; our kinsmen maintain and practise non-Islamic traditions and customs, and we are voiceless. Nearby our mansion a group of dissidents has built their own mosque; there they say Amen in a

Intizar Husain

loud voice, and here we practise the virtue of silence. Yes, also, Sheikh Sadeeq saheb brought news concerning you, announcing that you have built a new house for yourself, with a drawing room which has sofas and a television. We were delighted to hear that, and thanked God that you had made up your loss. Over here, the condition of the mansion is nothing to boast of: the already sagging beams sag even more after the last year's monsoon, and the roof of the living room is in such a state that when you look up you can see the sky. You very well know about our tight circumstances and debt. If you could manage to send some money, I will have a little repair work done on Father jani's grave. More than that, perhaps, is not advisable at the moment. The verdict has not come out yet regarding the mansion case. Honourable brother saheb handed over the case papers to me a little before passing away in '74. Thank God, I have handled every court appearance successfully since then, as I have always sought lawyers known for their credibility and experience. My hope is that the verdict, by the grace of God, will arrive soon, and in our favour. You cannot trust that the messenger of death will not decide to knock at the door of my life. Sometimes I grow extremely worried as to who will take care of the case after me.

Wherever I turn, I encounter nothing but darkness. Regarding our son, Akhtar, well, he has broken all rules of decency as he has adopted the name Premi and has become an actor for the radio and theatre. Moreover, junior brother marhoom's daughter, Khalida, has married a Hindu advocate, and wears a sari quite shamelessly, displaying a bindi on her forehead. And the picture of our family in Pakistan is a story you must know better than I. I have had the misfortune to hear that sister jani's daughter has settled into a marriage of her own choice, and that too with a man of the Wahabi faith! Above all, sister jani herself, I have learned to my dismay, has no qualms about sitting in the car unveiled and buys fabric dealing face to face with the cloth-sellers.

I was fated to live and be a witness to all of that. Senior bhai saheb marhoom and junior bhai, both, took their leave in good times. When I venture to the graveyard and offer prayers at father jani's and junior bhai's graves, I remember and miss dear elder brother saheb with a sharp ache in my heart. What cruel times have befallen us that no one can even go and offer prayers at his grave. The very family that lived and died in one place now has its graves scattered across three graveyards. I had very respectfully requested bhai saheb that if he must leave us then he should join Kamran mian in Karachi. But his love for the younger son took him to Dhaka. His untimely death was a great shock to us, though now that I reflect, I am of the opinion that there were reasons why God took him away so early. He had a pious soul. Nature did not consent that he live through the days of humiliation and pain. I, the sinner, was chosen to carry that cross.

Now since the shadow of the elders does not protect me, and our family has been divided up and scattered across India, Pakistan and Bangladesh, and I myself am sitting at the mouth of the grave, I cannot help feeling that what I have been entrusted with should now be handed over to you, for you will soon be the heir of the family, yet what I wish to hand over to you can be handed over through memory only. Honourable brother saheb took with him to Dhaka the mementoes of the village including the family tree, and wherever the members of our family were stolen from us by the tide of time, those mementoes followed suit. Imran mian came to us empty-handed. The gravest tragedy is the loss of the family tree. Our ancestors, who carried the blood of the great Sadaats in their veins, have endured great suffering and trials, still it is I who was chosen to bear the shameful tragedy of the loss of our pedigree. We are now a family afflicted with suffering, one that has lost its nest and its pedigree, and is a victim of disorder; if one member was destroyed in India, another perished in Bangladesh, and the next chased dust in Pakistan. Our faith has been ruptured, as some of us have accepted non-Islamic ways of life, and are marrying into other religions. If the drift continues, then our true race will soon dwindle to extinction and nobody will be left to tell who we were and what we were.

Intizar Husain

So, our child! Listen: we are doubly noble Sayyads; and our lineage can be traced back to Hazrat Imam Musa Kazim.

We are Muslims of the just faith of Hanafi. We believe in the Companions of the Prophet and maintain a deep affection for the Prophet's family. Father jani observed the practice of fasting on the day of Ashur and all day he would remain sitting on the prayer mat. There was a rosary in our house which turned crimson at the time of the afternoon prayer every day. Father jani used to tell us that the rosary beads had been made from the very soil of the precious earthen floor where the first mortal of our family, Hazrat Imam Husain, peace be upon him, was brought down from his horse. With the reddening of the rosary, father Marhoom's contemplative state would deepen, but he refrained from flagellation and weeping, for that is non-Islamic, he maintained. But, yes, he would have cauldrons of khichde cooked and distributed among the poor and homeless. Then, after Partition, only a single cauldron was left behind. However, last year we lost that too. This year we managed to have one cauldron of rice-lentil cooked; what follows next year, only God knows. Inflation is soaring unchecked and our situation grows more and more fragile. Son, though we don't know at what rate onions are selling in Pakistan these days, what we do know is that once prices go up they don't come down easily, and once ethics plummet they don't right themselves again. All I have as a word of advice is to pray, all of us, that the day never comes. And if such a calamity does indeed come upon us, then we mortals must ask for forgiveness and recite the Holy Quran, since there are clear guidelines in the story of A'ad and Samood for those who possess wisdom.

Anyway, I was speaking of our family, the family whom I have seen gathered in one place and then disintegrate before my eyes. You hardly saw the family together, however, and witnessed the disintegration a lot more. Having us sit around him, Father jani once addressed his wish to us—the three brothers—that God might keep his grave fragrant with the haar-singhaar tree. He used to recount to me that his father, honourable Sayyad Hatim Ali, had spoken to him moments before expiring saying that his father, honourable Sayyad Rustom Ali, told him one day about something that contained every important anecdote of our family but was lost in the turmoil of 1857 when he and his family had to abandon their home at 24 Khwaja and drift from desert to desert like beggars for years to come. And so I reveal to you today, relying on our elders' words that we in essence are the soil of Isfahan. Our earliest ancestor was Mir Mansur the recounter of the hadiths, who sold dates to earn his bread and his knowledge of the hadiths was like an ocean without shores. When the landless king Humayan sought refuge with his army in his city, it was then that he said farewell to Isfahan nisf-jahan, the half-world, to become the king's journey-mate. And became, after reaching the house of darkness of Hind, the minaret of the Faith's light. His shrine stands in Akbarabad to this very day. The grave, however, is earthen, not cemented. The virgins still come by to take a handful of the earth, securing it inside the knot of their dupattas ; they return, when expecting, to offer a linen on the grave. It was in the time of Shah Jahan that his children took the journey to reach Jahanabad. Then in the calamity of 1857 our ancestor Rustom Ali carried nothing when he fled from the city, not a single coin of money, only our family tree which he wrapped inside a kamarband around his waist. He also carried with him under his armpit a packet containing important papers and family records. But he had to fight the bandits on the way, and the papers in the packet fell out and were scattered in the confusion. He lost a few and was able to recover some, and among the lost ones was the family chronicles, but thank God a hundred times over not a word of the pedigree was stained.

After playing with dust for years he happened to pass by this very community finally, where your lone chacha now counts his last days. Finding this land kind-hearted, he pitched his life's tent here. Have it known that when the land is kind it is soft as the beloved's embrace and spacious as the mother's lap; but the

Intizar Husain

moment it turns unkind it is cruel as a heartless ruler and narrow as a jealous heart. The truth is that this land showered its kindness on us for years. For years it sheltered our flourishing stock in its lap the way a god-fearing mother would hold her children to her chest, not letting a single one out of her sight. Only three members of the family have dared venture out of sight before the Partition: bhai Ashraf Ali, bhayya Farooq and Payyare mian. Bhai Ashraf Ali was our chacha jani's son and was a year older than honourable brother jani and by virtue of that relation he was your tayaji. By the grace of Allah, he was a Deputy Collector, doing most of his duty time in distant districts. But he received all his mail at this address. Farooq bhai was his younger brother and my age. He worked in the Forestry Department and spent most of his life in the Central Provinces. All the woodwork and furniture you saw in our house was sent by him, or made to his order. Both brothers were the pride of the family. As you know they spent most of their lives away, yet, in the end, they returned to rest in their own soil.

Dear brother was phuphi amma's favourite, but that favouritism spoiled him so much that he began indulging in each of the seven vices. He was the first in our family to fall prey to the biscope. Once he was able to sway me to come along too, and my heart was out of control seeing Madhuri, but I controlled myself and never went in that direction again. Brother saheb was already an avid fan of theatre, and when the biscope came into town he fell head over heels in love with it.

Then he gave his heart to Salochna after watching *Bombai ki Billi* and then, stealing phuphi amma's gold earrings, he left home and went straight to Bombay. Father jani sent word, Son, you are not allowed to return. A rope-dancer duped him by saying she would introduce him to Salochna, and though she did not keep her word, she herself clung to him like bad news. He wasted his entire life in Bombay, only to come back to phuphi amma's funeral, and then as an old man with a long white beard, a rosary in hand, he wept his heart out at his mother's loss. We all pleaded with him to stay, but he replied, 'How could I . . . without father jani's permission.' Well, father jani had passed away a while back, so who was going to give the permission now! He returned to Bombay. The year 1947 had set in, and tragic incidents were occurring on the trains; everyone tried to reason with him, but he remained defiant and took the train. He did not reach Bombay, and who knows what misfortune befell him!

Payyare mian was the first member of our family whose life was claimed by the riots. I have kept a record of important figures and counts: thirty-one members of our family have passed away to this date. Nine died a natural death, and one drifted off from our lives and was lost to us. Twenty-one were murdered, seven of them were martyred by the keepers of the Hindu faith, while the remaining fourteen said farewell to us at the hands of the brothers of Islam in Pakistan, and one among those was shot dead by Ayub Khan's men for the crime of supporting Lady Fatima Jinnah in the elections. The other ten were killed in East Pakistan. I have been careful not to include Imran mian among those. Man must never give up faith in God's benevolence. My heart tells me that this piece-of-our-liver, if he has not reached Karachi yet, must be safe in Kathmandu, for the word Kathmandu reminds me that Farooq bhai's son, Sharafat, too, passed by here, after he managed to escape from Dhaka. He is Payyare mian's spit and image. The trauma had to have taken some toll on him, although while he stayed with us, he frequented the biscope without any fear, and when he was ready to leave, he left not for Kathmandu but for Bombay. When I questioned him regarding his odd choice of destination, he answered that he would meet Rajesh Khanna there. I said, O faithless fool, Rajesh Khanna is really not what you would call E. Billimoria or D. Billimoria that you are that restless to meet him, yet my words went in one ear and exited the other, and off he went to Bombay. But we got a letter from him about his well-being written from Lanka. Who knows how he ended up wandering there!

We had expressed our gratitude to God on seeing Sharafat, but our hearts were saddened beyond words when we learned of

Intizar Husain

his ways. Whatever has so far come to my ears suggests that our women have become more independent. Whichever woman I hear about, I hear that she has entered a marriage of her own choice. Before the Partition there had been only one incident which had the potential to defame the name of our family, and even that one was hushed up with great skill. A pebble once landed on the choti phuphi's roof, and as you know quite well that the falling of a pebble in the veranda or a kite's dipping down over the roof of a house where a girl is reaching her puberty is not taken as a good omen. Those days younger phuphi's older daughter was reaching that stage. The younger phuphi mentioned the incident to mian jani, producing the pebble along with the letter that had landed on the roof. Mian jani lost his temper and thundered, Raza Ali's son had the nerve to throw a pebble on our roof! But when younger phuphi reasoned with him and showed him the various pitfalls of the situation, only then did he calm down. Now they were left with not much choice except to marry the girl off to that good-for-nothing boy. Raza Ali could not have even dreamed of making a girl from such a family his daughter-in-law one day. He instantly agreed to the marriage, but insisted that the reading of the nikah should be in accordance with the tradition of his elders. Mian jani swallowed the insult; what else could he do? He gave his assent. But the result of that, we see today, is that Khadija's offspring are half-partridge and half-quail. One gives an offering of food on the holy eleventh, the other mourns in the Muharram. Well, then again, our entire family can now be considered half-partridge half-quail, and each one of us is a mourner for we have lost our pedigree and also the wisdom of knowing who we were. How will this family be set apart from other families in the future! This family of ours is a family in name only, for we are fallen leaves from a tree, falling to the whim of the wind, fated to the dust.

Beloved one! I am the mourner, here and now, of those fallen leaves. I recall the days when the family was a tree laden with fruit and leaves, and that inspires me to also count the gypsy leaves. I have kept a record not only of the deceased ones but of the living as well, writing down everyone's name, address, my impressions of them, and so on. I have researched which member of the family is still loafing about and in which country; also which relative of ours has made which country his home. I will soon mail this letter full of advice to you. I cannot count on myself anymore for I am a dawn's candle, soon to be extinguished with the closing of my eyes. You are the new eye and light of this dark-fated family, and if you attempt to bring the ones that have veered off the straight path back to light, it would be because you were blessed with obedience. Yet my observation tells me that once straws scatter they scatter for ever. One has never seen a dispersed family come back together. Still, one is obligated to try. Be the beacon of this helpless family and keep an eye on the vagabond types. We hear they might be easing the travel restrictions, and if that is so we hope you will make a journey our way as well. Let us see your face. Your chachi insists that you bring your wife along. Yes, that is right, don't come alone, and thus we shall be able to see your children's faces too. Who is dark and who is fair! One more thing: the details that I have penned regarding the growth in the numbers of our family members is currently restricted to their names; nothing about the qualities of their features and expressions has found space. You are advised to take care of that. Why don't you do this: send me a detailed list of the persons on your side who have expired, and also of those who were born. I find it difficult having to write a separate letter to each and every one of you. Though the mail can be sent and received, even a small postcard is costlier than sending a telegram. And what is this I hear? That Khadija's younger daughter is asking for a divorce, and is working with the family planning office? She has failed in her own life and now wants to break up others marriages as well. Yes, child, the family tree is lost; now, whatever this family may do does not surprise me. But I hear that other families are even a few steps ahead of us. Someone was telling me that Ibrahim has erected

Intizar Husain

another factory by selling impure flour, and look at Mian Fiazuddin, who used to wander the lanes here in ragged clothes and has now built houses with black money. I ask, has every family lost its pedigree in Pakistan? Strange! We have spent centuries in the land of Hind, some of it in a time of grandeur and pride, some in decline. Allah is great! He made us rule the land and He made us the ruled as well. We kept the family tree dearer than life. But the members on your side lost it in a quarter century. Still and all, God bless them!

How much more can I write! Though I could go on for ever, you should be content with whatever I have managed to write. Send us a word of your welfare, and inform us when you are coming. Let me finish the letter now because the prayer time is approaching. And after that I have to arrange the case papers. There is another court appearance tomorrow. This will be the four hundred and twenty-seventh appearance. Just like in the past, by the grace of God, this too will be attended gracefully. Perhaps it is for these court appearances that I am still alive; otherwise there is nothing left in your old chacha, not even the desire to live. Coming into the world, I saw many things, even what I did not have to see. Now I pray for my eyes to close soon so I will see what I have been desiring to see for a long time.

Your chacha, desirous of His protection

Nameless Qurban Ali
Dated, 27 Ramzan ul Mubarik, h 1394
Corresponding to 15 October 1974

—Translated from the Urdu by Moazzam Sheikh

in his own time

Talat Abbasi

At the group home in Harlem I am given the usual royal welcome. Omar, of course, heads the procession of half a dozen friends hurtling towards the front door to welcome the visitor at Sunday lunchtime. I laugh and step back instinctively, throwing out a hand to fend off the rising forest of arms towards me. I am touched, amused, overwhelmed. Denise who opens the door is adept at handling this. One word from her—'back'—and they immediately vanish into the living room in front of the TV. Fame is fickle, I am forgotten instantly. I am just a part of the Sunday ritual, have been for ten years, Omar's mom with his lunch. Omar alone remains behind, my hand imprisoned in his vice-like grip.

'Lucky Omar!' says Denise, giving him a playful shove towards the kitchen. Lucky. A strange word to use for Omar, for any of them for that matter but I know what she means. I've heard it so often from her and her colleagues. Omar is lucky because his mother visits him so often. I don't question this assertion, don't ask about the others. I don't need to. The visitors' sign-in book is thick with sheets—most of all with my own signature. I want to tell her with some pride that it's partly cultural, that Asian families are generally among the closest, that's all. But I don't want to start a discussion which may offend anyone. And I don't want to ever offend anyone who has anything at all to do with Omar for fear of—I'm not sure what—just a generalized paranoia. The home is called Mercy House. No misnomer that, that's what they all need—and from strangers, there's the rub of it.

'They get excited because of *him!*' grumbles Denise handing me Omar's plate with its guard. 'Jumping up and down, running to the window. Really loves his mom, this one. The way he waits for the doorbell and watches out for you. And only on Sundays mind you. Never Saturday. Understands the difference. Amazing, isn't it?'

An achievement certainly, I think, for one who is a stranger to the alphabet, to numbers, to time as measured in any way, by the hour or the day.

The visit begins in the basement with another ritual. This one, a tussle between Omar and me, is a formality because I know which way it's going to end. Year after year I have tried to teach him how to kiss, how to simply touch my cheek with his lips, nothing more, let's not even burden him with the kissing sound. And Omar has made some progress. He has learned to suffer my kisses. A lifetime's experience has resigned him to some of his mother's strange ways, her singular needs. Kissing him is one of them. So now he submits to a rain of kisses on his forehead and cheeks. But today, too, filial duty, patience and indulgence all reach their limits. So when I offer him my cheek and try to pull his head down to it, pursing my lips to show him how, he pushes me into the plastic chair at one end of the card table. I hear clearly this reminder of *my* duties and start to lay out the banquet.

'Okay Omar,' I say.

In his own way and in his own time, I used to think. But now he's seventeen, surely past the age for kissing lessons by any standard. Yet they continue because it's just so hard sometimes to be a 'normal' person, to think outside the limits of the box where love and kisses always go together. I won't be disappointed though, if he never obliges because I am certain he loves me more than my cooking. And that, let me tell you, is saying a great deal. For twelve years, ever since he came to this country, he has loved America passionately—for Kentucky Fried Chicken (crispy style).

'He'll eat it at breakfast, lunch and dinner!' marvels Denise. 'Not just his own share, mind you, but everyone else's too!'

But just watch him set aside KFC for my kababs, my samosas, my parathas. All these he has consumed today and with a piece of the paratha is wiping his plate clean, a subcontinental habit I can't help wishing he'd unlearn. Another one he will not discard—to the consternation of the teachers in his day programme—is at least a full hour's siesta immediately after lunch. They've tried everything American—tuna salad, grilled cheese, hamburger—they all come laced with sleeping potions. And at every conference with his teachers I am given to understand that multiculturalism is being strained to its limits in this tolerant land.

But today he's behaving in a way I simply do not understand. He will not go to the sofa to sleep nor let me leave my chair. He is down on his knees trying to get my sneakers off. I can't imagine why and I tell him to stop several times. But at that he starts to whimper so I fall silent. Let him have his way. In fact why not join the game and help him because he really doesn't have the skill to undo shoelaces. But he pushes my hand away. Whatever he must do, it seems, he must do himself. I watch helplessly as his agitation increases, incomprehensible mutterings escaping him. He is close to tears in frustration when suddenly one shoe is off! The sock is slipped off easily. Then he raises his head, makes direct eye contact with me which he has learned to do increasingly well. He smiles a secretive smile. He draws a deep breath. I do too; the excitement is infectious. Then to my amazement my foot is carried to his lips, a feather grazes its sole.

I smile back. I understand it all. In his own way and in his own time, Omar has learned how to kiss.

Talat Abbasi

spots

Zahur-ul-Haq Sheikh

Inside the teacup, in the tea itself, in the air, hands, fingers, on the tables—wherever you look you see a spot. Filthy, delicious, stinking, dark red, darker, moving, in tatters, the spot hovered over his mind.

'Unhu.' As though he was about to throw up.

'This seems to be touching my lips,' and then his lips came into action to kiss it.

He saw, before his eyes, a mountain cave approaching him.

'The spot, unh, unhu,' again he felt like throwing up.

'Absolutely. You are right. That spot will cling to my character for ever,' his companion had heard the word 'spot' from his mouth.

'Where are we all headed, dear? Which way?' he said and then, closing his eyes, sipped his tea.

'The tea tastes strange today.' He was beginning to hate the tea. 'Yuck! And there's a smell coming from the tea as well,' he thought silently.

'Why, has it become cold?' his companion asked, but he remained silent.

'A smell,' he thought. '. . . begins to feel quite pleasing to me sometimes.' He continued to think as he stroked his pallet with his tongue.

Originally published as 'Dhabbey' in *Savera*, Issue 42, 1990, Lahore

And then he noticed a completely separate spot, over there in the dense forest of Changa Manga. A bamboo mat was spread on one side, a transistor radio right beside it, followed by piles of orange peels and chewed sugarcane pieces near a basket. No one sees the place, nor can anyone head in that direction. There is a box of sweetmeats next to the mat. There is a packet containing chicken tikka and roast, and then a blur is opening the box. Jaidi has reclined in front of him.

'Their pastry is quite delicious, isn't it?' he said sucking his own lips. 'Ah-ha, that's lovely,' he thought. 'That's how you kiss,' addressing himself.

'You were very brave. I am surprised, rather happy after listening to this.' He adjusted his pants and, placing one leg over the other, renewed, 'One's dignity is more important.'

'Yes, thank God,' said Jaidi and ordered another round of tea.

'Jaidi, don't ask how sad it made me listening to your tale,' trying to smell something in the air, 'but how did you find out?'

'Well, I suspected something as we sat in the car. Credit it to my good luck. It was meant to be so.'

'But you? . . . You can jump? . . . What I mean is that you showed tremendous courage.' Both fell silent.

'Wow, so you jumped off,' he said again.

'Almost.'

'This happened in the morning or evening?' he asked, blinking.

'Morning, brother. Like I said I thought they had a morning plan like we gather at the Shezan in the evenings.'

'I see,' he said.

'But why do you seem worried all of a sudden?' Jaidi asked.

'No, no . . . really, man. Well, your story has that effect.' He shook his head with some force this time.

'Even beauty is a sin in this world,' Jaidi said.

'Sick people, the whole lot. Though not everyone is like them,' he responded. 'Then I am sick too; what the hell am I thinking?' He scolded himself.

The tea arrived in the meantime.

Although the friendship between Shaukat and Jaidi was quite new, they were becoming close pretty fast. Every evening they came to the Indus to have tea. Along with the conversation concerning the world they would touch upon each other's lives as well. So when they met this evening, Shaukat asked Jaidi rather suddenly:

'Man, you used to be quite close to Abdul. But lately I haven't seen you two together.'

'Don't ask, Shaukat dear.'

'But he seems to be sputtering all kinds of filth.'

'Lies, all lies.'

'That sure is, but I'd like to hear your side, too.'

Another round of tea in the meantime. Jaidi began narrating his tale as he made the tea.

'What happened was that Abdul and I became friends through Aslam. The same Aslam who ran off with my money. And, sir, I sensed that Mr Abdul carried a strange attitude. In fact he would go on staring at me and addressing me in a vulgar way. I didn't like him much, but since we hung out in the same company I didn't say anything. And I wasn't on good terms with Saleem and the gang either. They too weren't decent folks. They get the crown for the art of accusation. Yes, let them go to hell, but take a look at Mr Abdul's feat. He'd stare at me incessantly, but I would remain quiet. He wouldn't let go of it. One day, really out of jest, I made the mistake of calling him a homo. He hit the ceiling. His face turned red and his eyes popped out with anger.' Jaidi wiped the sweat off his face as his sipped the tea.

'Yes, and then?' Shaukat said.

'Then . . . man, I say let's forget this story. Let's pick up some other thread,' Jaidi suggested.

'But I want to find out what's behind his rubbish?'

'Well, sir . . . I told you he got mad for no reason at all. I really had no idea. But he harboured it in his heart. I thought we had put the matter to rest. But he . . . see it this way, he found an excuse to carry out his cheap behaviour. He gathered a few men and planned to kidnap me. One feels ashamed, Shauki brother, even narrating such tales . . .'

'Really—what an asshole he is.'

'He said, "Now I'll show you what a homo is." '

'Such ugly thoughts he has, the rascal,' thought Shaukat, considering something, and then he began seeing spots and more spots everywhere, dark red spots, darker spots, moving, spots in tatters, inside the teacup, in the tea itself, in the air, on his hands, fingers, on the tables, in all the four directions.

'A real motherfucker that Abdul is—he is Mr Incredible,' he thought silently.

'Where was he taking you?' he asked.

'Changa Manga.'

'He seems to be enjoying it,' he said in his heart.

He served one cup to Jaidi and kept the other for himself, when the tea arrived. During this time they both remained quiet.

'No, no, he calls me brother. But what difference does that make? That's bad,' he thought, as he licked his lips.

'Yuck,' came out of his mouth.

'You only say "yuck" and there are those who in fact do such things,' said Jaidi.

'Assholes! Let them go to hell.' He started tapping on the table with a spoon.

As they finished the tea, Jaidi said, 'Come, Shaukat, let's go out somewhere.'

'Where?'

'Let's just drive around; I am feeling a bit melancholic.'

'So be it,' said Shauki. 'Thank God, I'll be able to get out of a world full of spots.' He breathed a sigh of relief.

They paid the bill and came out of the restaurant. Jaidi started the car and soon they left the city behind.

'Shaukat, I wonder sometimes how mean the world is.'

'Don't start now,' he replied. 'Mean, *mean*—such a delicious word,' he seemed to be hearing it in his heart.

'Look at it. He slandered me for no reason.'

'Hey, hey, look straight, we still need you.' Jaidi barely avoided an accident.

'Man . . . I am quite upset.'

'Yes, my friend, you have a reason to be.'

'Is there a solution?'

'Solution! I say let him bark his guts out; he'll be quiet eventually.'

'Shaukat, Jaidi's heart wants it quits.'

'Come on. You don't need to take it to heart.'

Shaukat bit his lips. 'My dear . . . just, now . . . leave it.' He looked out of the car window, thinking. 'Darkness. Ah, what an amazing thing darkness is. He seems quite cunning to me . . . quite sexy he is, a roamer.'

Jaidi suddenly stopped the car. Shaukat came out of his reverie. He looked towards Jaidi, who rested his head against the wheel.

'But it is full of spots.' He looked with amazement.

'Jaidi, Jaidi . . . why aren't you talking!' and Jaidi didn't move a muscle.

'He's been treated unfairly. He's a good boy, yes good . . . boy, what a wonderful thing boy is! What a lovely word!' Shaukat went on speaking to himself. Jaidi still had his head on the wheel.

'Hear me out. Let them go to hell,' Shaukat shook him again, quite irritated inwardly. 'God alone knows what mess I have got myself in today.' He wiped his sweat.

'I'll have Abdul murdered,' Jaidi sprang suddenly, slapped his forehead, resting his head against his palm this time.

'Murder . . . Murderer, that you are indeed . . . Heartless . . . What my heart yearns is to kiss you,' Shaukat thought as he gazed at him. Shaukat's heart quickened.

'Shauki, I'll scar my face someday.'

'You've gone nuts,' he responded. 'Nuts, crazy yes, oh yes nuts,' he repeated silently. 'OK, Let's drive now. Bravo.' He patted Jaidi.

'He's only concerned with himself,' Shauki ground his teeth, pulling the fingers of his hand with the other.

'Shaukat, my friend . . .'

'Move on, dear. It is getting late. Let's head back.' He acted cold. 'Shaukat, my foot. What an ass!!' He cursed Jaidi in his heart.

'Shaukat, I have not been able to find a companion whom I can trust.'

'Companion, silly . . . I . . . am I . . . not your companion?'

'Shaukat, you, I mean you? Of course, yes, oh dear, don't deceive me.'

'Deceive . . . deceive,' Shaukat repeated the word unconsciously.

'Shaukat, look, seriously. Don't deceive,' and Jaidi choked.

'Hey, you're crying . . . goofball.' Moving closer, Shaukat wiped the tears with his handkerchief.

'Look, I have money, intelligence, ability, and respect as well. God has blessed me with everything. The only thing missing is a friend. Don't know why that is so.'

'And me, not even me?'

'You . . . yes, yes . . . you are . . . I feel you are,' and Jaidi pulled him closer.

'Shaukat, should I tell you one thing?'

'Yes?'

'We are all alone,' and Jaidi rested his head on his shoulder.

'Jaidi, not that again. If you don't stop saying that, move away then.'

'No, no, for God's sake. That's not what I'd meant.' Jaidi peered into his eyes.

'Meant or not . . . what is it to me? What swamp have you dragged me in? Muck, a delicious muck it is. But no, no,' Shaukat was lost in thought. A few minutes later he jabbed Jaidi's cheek with his fist playfully.

'OK. Please, drive the car; we're getting late.' He helped Jaidi sit up straight after a few moments passed.

The car drove on. He stuck his face out of the car's side window to look out as he felt the puffs of cold wind. There was darkness everywhere; he pulled his face in quickly.

'Who is that flying in the air? Those are really weird-looking shapes. It seems someone's put spots all over the air. No, they are not locusts, but look like worms of a sort. Of different colours.' He shook his head as he rolled up the window.

'What's happening to me today?' he pondered while biting his nails.

'Jaidi, what the hell is that out there?'

'Nothing. Only fields.'

'Wow, look how far we have come out!'

'Move faster.'

'You are moving slowly, slowly.'

'Slowly, slowly?' and Jaidi didn't say a word after that. 'Slowly, slowly,' repeated Shaukat in the secrecy of his mind.

'What sort of circles are these? They look like worms to me. We should roast and eat them. Yes, finger-licking. Phew.' He looked at the darkness again.

'Strange weather today, Jaidi,' he broke the silence.

'Hey, you are crying, while driving the car?'

Jaidi stopped the car once again and leaned against Shaukat's shoulder.

'I am carrying a pile of sorrows, Shaukat. Do you know I have a stepmother, who's always scolding me. I feel trapped. I don't know what God has against me. Nor does my father care a hoot about me. Shaukat, I want you to throttle me, kill me. I have no companion. I'll kill myself. I don't have any friends. Nor do I need one.' Shaukat ran his fingers through Jaidi's hair after placing Jaidi's head on his thighs.

'Deceiving is bad, right? Yes, see, what if you also turned out to be the same? I'll be finished then. I don't have bad intentions. I can swear. Have me promise anything, or whatever you want, whatever you say, whenever,' Jaidi cried like a little kid.

'Oh . . .' as if Shauki was jolted out of his senses.

'Yes, oh-ho, you worry out of habit. You've got plenty of friends,' he reasoned with Jaidi and held on to his chin. 'You are such a child . . .' He touched his cheeks. 'Sweet child.'

'A strange smell is coming,' he sniffed around. 'Sometimes I like the smell of petrol. I feel the urge to gulp it down. Once in my childhood I'd liked muck. I had chewed it down. Filthy soil! But I don't know why it tasted so good.' Shaukat was lost in bizarre thoughts.

He looked up and rested his finger on Jaidi's lips.

'The touch of lips. Hey, there are spots on them, but how beautiful. How soft they are, soft and hot like meat, like the raw meat of a fawn.

'You too are deceiving me. Yes, yes, I can feel it. Leave me alone.'

'Nope.' Shaukat shook his head.

'Bad.'

'No, not bad.'

'Then say you are my brother.'

'I am.'

'Not like that. Say the whole thing, You are my brother.'

'Yes, even closer than brothers.' Shaukat patted his cheek. He looked around. The road was completely deserted.

The darkness seemed to be getting denser out there, and the circles formed everywhere. He considered the circles in such darkness quite absurd.

'Spots, oh-ho, I am thinking of spots again. No, there is no spot here. But there are. Come on, you spots! Come from all the four corners. I find pleasure in you. Sp . . . pots are mine, but what is it in my grip? I'll catch them, all the spots. Yes, with his help . . . He needs them. What a cute thing you are, you famished little being. Speechless,' he mused.

He urged Jaidi, 'You are crying, Jaidi. Silly, don't weep. Overcome the sorrow.'

Jaidi looked up. His eyes were closed.

'What are these, all around me, stars? But they all turned into a moon,' Shaukat was in a dream it seemed.

'Leave me, you filth, dirt!' Jaidi sizzled when he saw his face.

'I say leave me alone, you pile of filth!' Jaidi slapped Shaukat.

'Hey . . .' Shaukat stared at Jaidi wide-eyed. Jaidi sat covering his open mouth with his hand.

Shaukat massaged his cheek and, looking at Jaidi with his half-open eyes, smiled lightly.

'Forgive me, forgive me. You are very nice, right? Oh my brother, I have become very upset. I am a loony bin, yes, I have become one. You should just finish me off.' Soon Jaidi got hold of the front of Shaukat's shirt and was crying, choking.

'Tell me, have you forgiven me. Tell me now!' Jaidi went on repeating.

'Where did the moon go? Did it dive? No. It is right there. Yes, yes. I am melting, slipping, sliding. Time has arrived to go down. To float away. Into the moon, into the air below, the atmosphere, into the ether, the stains, the spots. The moon, the point, the circle, yes, yes, yes,' and he nodded ever so lightly.

On the other hand, Jaidi went on, 'Tell me, please, have you forgiven me? Speak or else I won't speak with you. Say something.' But he remained silent.

'Yes, bravo,' he said.

'Come closer to me; be a good boy, rather, yes, you . . . let's together go down the moon, the spot-filled moon, let's enter the spot. It's being pulled away somewhere. Yes, let me be pulled too; let me get hold of it.' He was sunk in thought again while Jaidi still wept.

'No, no, nothing's the matter,' he said to Jaidi and, leaning, kissed him.

'There is no difference between us, right?'

'No.'

'Not like this; say the entire thing, "There is no difference between us." '

'Yes . . .'

'You *are* very sweet, right?'

And a little while later Shaukat thought: 'The spots have moved farther away. The moon has hidden itself. The stars are forming again. Let them. What do I care.' Later as they approached the city, Jaidi dropped Shaukat at his place.

'We'll meet tomorrow.'

'We will meet tomorrow, right?' Jaidi repeated.

'Certainly,' said Shaukat, and Jaidi drove off in his car at full speed. Shauki watched him go. The fading car appeared to him like a spot.

—Translated from the Urdu by Moazzam Sheikh

mangoes in the time of winter

Ashu Lal

A t first glance it seemed as though both of Lala's eyes were
made of stone; only one was. From the moment you entered,
the Club suggested it might have been an extension of an old
building, and that was a fact. Just one wall separated the Club
from the building. The last few rains had forced the signboard of
the Club to lean against the wall. Even if you wiped the dust off
it, you couldn't read the words 'Nawab Health Club'.

The stranger hesitated a bit, then sat down next to Dr A.B.
Ghauri, a member of the Club for almost twenty years. They
called him Doctor because of his father, who had been the
Nawab's horse doctor long ago. The Dr. himself was employed
at the Deputy Commissioner's office. The stranger was introduced
to the Club for the first time as Doctor's guest. 'He is one of us!'
Doctor said as he introduced him to Lala, who then looked away,
though the stranger felt as if one eye still clung to him.

Arch after arch, not a single wall in the Club's dilapidated
veranda was spared; besides the posters of female wrestlers with
big behinds, a wall or two were plastered with pages cut out
from film sections of the newspapers. An old calendar celebrating
the Pride of the Wrestling World hung from a thick nail. On it
was the picture of the World Champion Bholu the Wrestler (with
his seven brothers), one hand holding the iron club, the other a

Originally published as 'Poh Manh De Amb' in *Pancham*, June-July, 2002,
Lahore

pillar. To the left of the wall, under the shelter, khoya was being prepared behind the haze of smoke. Right next to it, an old man (bare-chested, generous deposits of fat on his body glistening) was ploughing a spatula through the length of a large pan of milk as he rocked like an oil-mill, oblivious to the world around him, silent—no one knew his real name; only Lala had the courage to address him as 'Neck-squeezer'. Beside the shelter, there lay on the floor the exercise equipment: big, rusty iron discs glued to each other; springs; dumbbells; cords; hooks—all the equipment for working out was present under the tin shelter, but the gym was nowhere to be seen. The stranger whispered into the Doctor's ear:

'Where's the Club?'

'This is it, may you live long!'

Lala answered before Dr Ghauri could as if all this time he'd been keeping an eye on the stranger. How strange, he heard even my whisper! The stranger was surprised. 'It once was, may you live long!' After a pause Lala scooped out the barfi and arranged the pieces on a tray, sighing, 'Ahh . . . haaa . . .' and added, 'No one uses silver leaves anymore.'

'You tell him yourself,' Lala put the rest of the Club's story in Dr Ghauri's mouth, and with that, it seemed, he became completely at ease with the stranger's presence.

As the story would have it, the Club was in fact a part of Nawab Rais-ud-Daula's mansion, which his father had given as a gift to Lala's father, Hatu Khan the wrestler, which in turn metamorphosed—due to Lala and the younger Nawab's collusion—into a club. Nawab Rais immediately gave up exercising as he pulled a muscle, but Lala kept at it for a while. Then, gradually, the Club grew into Lala's storage for ghee and a factory to manufacture sweetmeats. That day Lala treated the newcomers to aphrodisiacal raw dates; the stranger couldn't understand why the barfi wasn't offered instead. This was his first encounter with Lala.

'He knows a few prescriptions as well!'

Pausing briefly, Doctor added to what he'd already said, gesturing with his hands as though they carried an invisible watermelon:

'It runs in the family . . . they are quite a renowned name!'

At the mention of 'renowned' Lala took another close look at the stranger and said, 'I'd already suspected so.'

Although everyday medicinal prescriptions were Lala's favourite topic, he liked, also, to touch on the issues of manliness, impotence and diabetes with any newcomer. Sprinkling a concoction of almonds and pistachios on the barfi in the tray, he admitted his weakness:

'I'll present you as well . . . a gift!'

'You won't forget the collyrium made with the essence of the mulberry tree. Trust me, your eyes won't water at all . . . despite the prick; that's what father used to say, may you live long!'

'The eyes of this city, after all, are quite dazzling!'

Although the stranger hadn't intended a tease, Lala winked his only eye in agreement, something which he rarely did. Then, the moment he popped a piece of white cashew in his mouth, he acted as though he hadn't heard anything.

If you looked at the eastern end of the Club, you'd see another building behind Nawab Rais-ud-Daula's two-hundred-year-old mansion. And just try and ask the inhabitants of the Nawab's neighbourhood here about the web of houses, no one would utter a word.

The stranger looked up casually to view the building; in the distance, he noticed a blur of Rajasthani pink umbrella-like domes.

'They won't crumble.'

Lala became conscious of the building's decrepit condition from the stranger's gaze and said, 'For fifty years this place has belonged to the pigeons!'

'The Club, however, came into existence only yesterday, may you live long!

'Let me tell you—This building belongs to the younger Nawab saheb. But during the killing of the Sikhs, the family of Nawab

Muzaffar Khan Saddoza'i of Multan took possession of one of the buildings here.' Then he whispered into the stranger's ear, 'By God, I saw the groom's carriage with my own eyes . . .'

Just as Lala had started the story, he lost his thread—because there seemed to be no logical connection between the killing of the Sikhs and the horse carriage.

'Father knows it all. He's got old books as well . . . I swear. 'Hand-written . . . because my father was the court wrestler. There was a library as well somewhere behind the royal dressing room, where, in the vacant area, we used to exercise as kids . . .' The stranger interrupted, 'Where is the library now?'

'That I don't know,' pretending to be unaware of it, he added, 'Father knows all . . . he's still living; if you like you can meet him. 'Ask Doctor. He even played with him when he was a kid.'

'How so?'

With that Lala balanced the sweetmeat tray on his palm and stood up, 'I'm off . . . my shop is just next door . . . Have some bhang, my friend—consider this your own Club. No, I don't drink this monster . . . They say it clouds the eye . . . ' Lala explained as he saw bhang being passed around, and moved on. Lala had hardly put his foot out the door when Beeba the Evil let loose his tongue which was famous for being a foot and seven inches long.

'The one drinking it, next to Nawab saheb, is my father . . .' as he touched his ears, 'God have mercy . . . bhang doesn't become the dark-skinned.'

The stranger's second meeting with Lala was at his faluda shop. The shop decked up with glinting glass was situated at the southern end of the goldsmith's bazaar. Treating them as friends, Lala didn't charge anyone for the faluda, yet slipped in, 'You get this tiny bit of cream for ten rupees . . . what, just one cup took care of your hunger?'

'Ah . . . ha, one can't really satisfy a heart's hunger.'

'Sugar, milk, ghee, butter, cream, no one can compete with your Lala, owing to your blessing, in the entire state. If any of your friends ever need pure ghee, just let me know. I'll sell it for a song!

'We still use the pure ghee at home . . . by God. Not once have I ever visited the hospital. Ask why . . .'

Lala kept wobbling his head.

'That's what Father taught me since childhood. Straight from home to the shop and from the shop to home. Eyes can't see now . . . ears can't hear. Let me tell you . . . Half my time was spent exercising and preparing the food . . . mostly this younger brother of mine sits here.' Saying this, he stepped down from the wooden platform along with the other four. Meanwhile, Lala's younger brother, a spitting image of him, took his place. From the front of the shop they hardly had to walk a hundred paces, through the labyrinthine lane, to reach the Club. During the walk Lala kept harping about his wrestling teachers, their tricks, and about the many feats of not having to burp even after devouring an entire lamb. His unease regarding the stranger was completely gone by now. And as he stepped across the Club's entrance door, he said, 'The entire equipment of the Club was given by brother Jhara of the Bholu family! I brought it myself from Lahore on the truck and . . . We are related to the Bholu family. Briefly, way back, I wrestled too. Ask Doctor . . . how it was.'

Lala asked for Doctor's backing as though he feared his narration somehow lacked conviction.

'Yes . . . certainly,' Doctor offered absent-mindedly.

Today Lala appeared even kinder than the first time.

If you want to know the truth, the Club is in fact Lala's sweetmeat factory and a place where he stores pure ghee. Here they boil milk down to khoya and fill up tray after tray of sohan halwa to bring it to the shop. Most of Lala's other activities take place in the Club. This is the time when the birds come as well. Among the visitors, Dr Ghauri is a daily fixture; the rest of the crowd is quite impressed by him, yet they are more in awe of Khan the DC. Although he is a mere police constable, the guys here refer to him as the DC—short for Deputy Commissioner.

He wears his uniform to the Club. Due to his potbelly he keeps his belt untied and a minimum of one bucket of bhang is needed for him every day.

Besides those two, the famous beloved 'Beeba the Evil' and 'Dedda the Daredevil' too are regular members of the Club. There is Nawab Rais-ud-Daula also, who along with Lala is the founding member; then you have a Colonel or two and a few intellectuals, who, since the failure of the revolution, show up here, repeating, *Glasnost, Glasnost!* Other stars of the Club refer to one of the intellectuals as '*bogeyman!*' behind his back. Upon Nawab saheb's request, 'Dedda the Daredevil' once pumped up his tiny muscles to intimidate them, but by now all the weapons of intimidation have been exhausted. The comrades make Nawab saheb feel extremely uncomfortable. If he happens to be at the Club, he gets up as soon as he spots them and sneaks out the secret door in the back that leads to his own mansion. Beeba the Evil is a butcher by profession. His butcher shop is right next to the Shahi Bazaar. He believes nobody is better than him in the art of carving meat in the entire state. 'You call him a butcher who lets a drop of blood stain his clothes? God's curse on him!'

That is his pet line. Besides being a butcher, he can wag his tongue like that of a barber, always complaining. Nawab saheb often tells him to his face in Urdu-soaked Siraiki:

'You stink of meat to me.'

Perhaps that's why the name Beeba the Evil has stuck to him. Every time Nawab saheb comes he hands out a few buds of jasmine and pods of cardamom to everyone. Nawab saheb thinks that Dr Ghauri, who was his own and Lala's classmate till the tenth grade, entertains dirty thoughts about him. So he always sits at a safe distance. The Club's cleanest spot is reserved for him.

In the course of his daily chatter Beeba the Evil reveals that Nawab saheb is terrified of lizards. It is his habit to stare at the lizards for half of the day and feel scared for the other half. Nawab saheb likes to dab a light make-up on his face when he comes to the Club and no one has ever seen him take off his red Turkish

Ashu Lal

cap. And he's also shown a peculiar weakness for wearing silky new clothes since childhood.

Beeba the butcher reveals in a secretive tone, also, that Nawab saheb regularly watches, everyday for an hour or two, his pigeons feeding on grain, playing around, and mating. And every once in a while, if his heart fancies he pretends to slap his servant lightly on the cheek. None of the Club members come here to do weights. Instead, it is the bhang that draws them here, but Lala himself has never tasted the bhang laden with the scent of almonds, poppy seeds, sesame, black pepper, and cardamom. Lala feels compelled to explain to each newcomer:

'I don't drink it . . . I swear!'

Yet they all know that he and Nawab saheb take opium . . . Lala looked to the stranger for a kind of validation, and asked:

'What about you?'

'I don't drink.'

The stranger noted the bhang being stirred with a piece of neem wood and shook his head. As he moved his cane stool, he slipped and realized the floor was greasy despite being washed every day.

'Be careful!'

Be careful . . . Lala had hardly uttered the warning when a boy of six or seven came rushing in uttering *daddy, daddy* . . . *daddy, daddy* and approached Lala, 'Daddy, daddy, mother says go and bring back two mangoes.'

'Be gone . . . you mama's boy.'

Looking away, Lala firmly pushed the boy aside and carefully phrased the words, 'The mistress of the house is thick-skulled, may you live long!' and ended up laughing with the rest as though this were a revelation. Indeed! The stranger started upon hearing the mention of mangoes in winter, so Lala grabbed him by the arm and said 'Come.'

Crossing the main veranda, then arriving at the back of another smaller one, Lala walked with the stranger to a room, which it seemed had not been opened for over a hundred years, and halted. The next room was a storage space for oil and ghee.

Lala opened the lock and the stranger noticed a full-sized refrigerator, as tall as Lala himself, standing in a corner of the room that was saturated with a light odour. The rest of the room was empty. Lala used a key to open the door to the freezer. The stranger was astonished to see the finest, paradisiacal mangoes filling up the freezer. Each mango had been placed separately, fresh as though recently plucked. Moreover, there were also five to seven tin boxes of pure honey with mangoes in them. As Lala closed the refrigerator he whispered secretively, 'The world is full of free-loaders, may you live long!'

'You'll get to taste it,' and turning the key three times he put it back in his pocket. The stranger followed Lala out of the room and found that bhang was being distilled.

'Catch the lion by the ear! Catch the lion by the ear!'*

Lala called out to the others, drawing attention, yet pretending to hide the mangoes like a child would. 'Serve halwa to our guest too,' Lala ordered Neck-squeezer. 'Only God knows whether he's going to give me the remedy or not.' How sweet the body of the tall and handsome Lala must be, the stranger had some idea by now, especially after having taken a look at the refrigerator, not to mention Lala's head which appeared to be visibly dyed black.

'I did not waste my life, may you live long! With your blessing, the entire state has seen my wrestler's loin-cloth!'

After a moment's reflection, he spoke, aided by hand gestures, 'You know where the Gujranwala Meat Karahi and Tandoori shop is located, right in front of the Medical College—that's where our gym used to be.'

Regardless of the fact that Lala himself never took part in wrestling, he still showed up wearing his wrestler's loin-cloth, his eyes highlighted with collyrium.

DC Khan brought the bucket to his mouth; the sound of drumbeats was heard in the distance. These were the remaining days of December. During this, Lala tricked the stranger into

---

* As *bhang* is being sifted, the holding of four corners of the cloth by four different men is referred to as catch the lion by the ear.

following him to a nook of the Club. He thought nobody noticed, but they all did. He offered, 'Let me reveal it, may you live long!' And with that he lifted his crumpled silken shirt up to show yellow stains the size of a quarter around the crotch of his cotton shalwar.

'Something keeps trickling all the time, I can't tell,' and letting his shirt down he added, 'You certainly have a remedy for this . . . whether you give it to me or not, that's your choice, may you live long!' With that both emerged from the corner. Fragments of the winter sunlight had washed over the tiny dome of the building after having just hopped over the walls of the Club. The stranger hesitated a bit, then spoke with equal secrecy.

'Let go of your loin-cloth, may you live long!'

—*Translated from the Siraiki by Moazzam Sheikh and Amna Ali*

the squatter

Asad Mohammad Khan

Babbar Khan peacefully stretched his legs lying beneath a bench made with wood and cast iron and gave up the ghost.

The last thought that entered his mind, before his neck rolled off to a side, was that of Dullichan lakhera, who writhed his last lying on the same bench. Right at that moment countless others were counting their last breaths, writhing. Babbar Khan thought the death was occurring all of a sudden; all Muslims of the city would certainly achieve the status of a martyr and by the grace of God find a place in the best of heaven. So, contentedly, Babbar Khan tried to recite the kalma-e shahadat and as usual got stuck half way.

It cannot be said with certainty whether he remembered the kalma-e shahadat correctly or not. So far he had survived by guessing since he had offered his shoulder to countless funerals and he knew that good manners demanded that one recite the kalma, which, except for a minor difference, was pretty much like the first kalma. He knew the first kalma perfectly by heart. But now that he was to read it on his own funeral it was crucial that he recite it right. 'This is not a moment for procrastination,' he thought. 'It's a matter of Salvation.' Right then the sound of gurgling came from above. It must be the same silly Dullichan gurgling. The case of these infidels is really a tough one. I ask

Originally published as 'Ghus Betthiya' in *Burj-e-Khamoshan*, Ibn-e-Hasan Press, 2002, Karachi for forgiveness. Forgive me, dear God. It is all right to sin, but idolatry and disbelief, I beg forgiveness!

There was another idol worshipper: Master Bhatnagar; with rotting teeth, the infidel; the pimp, always suggesting to me to have fun. 'Aye, what good getting educated would do for you, Mr Landlord? Have fun, fun, and more fun, you bastard puppy!'

Since now the matter of life itself was coming to an end, things and events poured into Babbar Yaar Khan's mind with clarity and sequence, yet the worldly sequence was not that orderly; there was some mix up. At some points whole decades were missing. For example he remembered the grubby-looking man he addressed as 'Miyan' wore soiled trousers and a coat tailored with the mushajjar fabric, as he entered the living room with a slant wearing red shoes. That man was indeed his father. Then everything got muddled up. Miyan's red shoes disappeared into non-existence. Only the coat of mushajjar remained behind in tatters which someone had turned into a book bag after unstitching and thoroughly washing it, and someone was beating the bag again and again with a very fine cane, which gave the sound of a firecracker. 'Aye, what good getting educated would do for you, Mr Landlord! Have fun, fun, and more fun, and still more, bastard puppy!'

So Babbar Khan had his fill having fun, meaning he didn't learn a single word beyond fourth grade. He roamed to his heart's content, went on hunting sprees, committed all kinds of frauds and lived through hard times, contracted syphilis and was disinherited. But these events had not taken place in this order. He was disinherited first. He was told since his father had died while the grandfather was still alive, then, according to the inheritance law and the sharia in Islam he had no rightful claim to the inheritance. Moreover, Babbar Khan might have sprouted from Zafar Yaar Khan's sperm (since the two had a tremendous resemblance), but was there any proof the woman known to be Babbar Khan's mother might have also been married to Zafar Yaar Khan? Secondly, when was she among the nobles? Before coming into Zafar Yaar Khan's service, she used to be called by the name of Jumrat. It does not make a bit of difference if the lowly of the lowliest were given the appellation of middle daughter-in-law or have her addressed as Farrukh Zamani Begum, she was and will remain Jumrat. And if you still insist on the legality of the issue, then provide us with a marriage certificate, witnesses and some other proof to nip the quarrel in the bud. What is the point in sitting shrunken-faced? Do you understand? Now go and have fun, understand? Go and have fun somewhere else, bastard puppy! Squatter! Why the hell have you popped up here to spoil our family tree?

It is difficult to enumerate here the things which lent a hand in turning Babbar Yaar Khan into a bastard puppy and a squatter. What little can be said in passing is that he was too young and his cousins were adults with a firm footing and mothers from influential families. Some of the cousins were beyond adulthood, clad in sherwani made of the serge fabric, and offered greetings to the Raja by making a full bow. Moreover, the other relatives and respected elders were frightened transvestites, who protected their mothers' marriage certificate inside a wax cloth and each one of them had permanently settled his bottom atop his property and were busy eating bread dipped in lard. They had no inclination to show solidarity with the squatter for no reason at all and invite the wrath of well-established, strong people for the sake of God. 'Brother, you decide: did the doctor prescribe that we cultivate enmity for a twelve-year-old orphan? This is not the British government. This is a Rajwara, sir. Dead bodies can be thrown into the Hallali canal in the night and made into ground meat to feed the dogs. We intend on being alive still. Do you understand, brother?'

What can be the reach of a twelve-year-old Babbar Yaar Khan? So an entire decade of his life completely phased out on hearing, Bring the proof of your mother's marriage, illegitimate child! Then think of living here. No one knows who he left the city with, and settled in a nearby village. Some contractor by the name of Rehmat-ul-lah had an out-of-use farm. When he returned from the city, he saw Babbar Yaar Khan eating wild fruits and picking wood. Noticing his built and wide forehead in contrast with the age, Rehmat-ul-lah hired him for basic food and a little money. It is here, as he reached to be twenty, that he first came to be called Babbara, later Babban Bhaiya. From taking care of the animals' dung to subduing the tribal servant women for the contractor from time to time all fell on Babban Bhaiya's shoulders. He woke up before dawn and set about conducting the farm. All day long, he would sing something in his painful voice. He encouraged the farmers to plough and enticed the crops to grow, and once, after he returned from the fields, when the village had gathered and master Siddeeq had arrived with his troupe he had sung along with his harmonium's weeping notes:

When the light of the love's candle will dim
I will set my heart on fire to make more light

Babbar Yaar Khan could not break out of a fit of choking as he wept: the reason being Babbar Yaar Khan had attempted to recognize, for the first time, during this season of spring, a difference between adultery and love, and in this attempt the child-widow, the daughter of Lala-ji of Chandanpura, got pregnant. The whole thing had turned too complex, because the contractor was of the opinion that any matter relating to Lala's daughter might very well cause him to wash his hands off his good name and farm. This worthless child-widow could as well have Rehmat-ul-lah ruined if an arrow shot in the dark by the contractor had not found perfectly Babbar Yaar Khan's chest melting with love. He spilled everything within three, four questions.

'Yes, he is in true love with the daughter of Lala of Chandanpura.'

'Yes, he intends to bring her into wedlock by converting her to Islam.'

'Of course, she has showed up at the threshing-floor every now and then.'

Rehmat-ul-lah the contractor took a sigh of relief and captured Babbar Yaar Khan with the help of the fellow villagers and tied him by the tree, then gave him such a thrashing with a cane that even the Thakur himself had to intercede, The bastard will die— untie the motherfucker. And they untied the motherfucker and tossed him out on the government road.

A process unfolded on Babbar Yaar Khan, after he was picked up from the government road, which usually unfolds on resource-less people, who have no caretaker and who have thoroughly been used up. Also, Babbar Yaar Khan had great injuries. And perhaps he had hurt his kidneys. Blood came with urine for a few days, later even the urine stopped. Anyway, the gypsies who picked him up off the road made him drink white tap-root and black tap-root and covered him with ointments, enabling him to progress from lying down to sitting position. Finally he was able to stand up and gradually began walking.

Time too began whistling and gliding lazily over Babbar Yaar Khan like a big steam-roller.

Babbar Yaar Khan set up a hut on a little hill away from the city. He began working. Then he got himself a woman, who turned out to be barren, and that is why it never went far enough to produce tiny little bastard puppies year after year. A short time later first the woman became ill as Babbar Yaar Khan looked after her with the bottom of his heart, even cleaning after her shit and puke; then he himself succumbed. The woman ran away with someone; and when he recovered finally, another woman felt pity on him and took him in. That woman used to live in the next-door hut and provided comfort at night to the labourers who worked at the mill; that is how she earned her bread. While living with the woman, his clothes first became dirty, then ragged. The woman got him a suit made with the markeen fabric and a cap of hard velvet bought with the money earned from having sex with the labourers. Babbar Yaar Khan dragged himself on his weak legs up the hill to the dilapidated eidgaah and offered two bits of prayer, thanking God for being alive.

A s a d   M o h a m m a d   K h a n

In the coming days he was as much alive as a vegetable is by clinging to the earth, because he had caught syphilis from the woman who slept around with the mill workers; and he had taken to getting high as well every second, third day; and now he could not muster enough strength to do any kind of labour. On top of everything else, he had learned quite a few tricks now of making dough. Theft was one important trick among them. Police had taken him away a few times also. The unfortunate people had put down Babbar Yaar Khan's name in their register as Babban son of Japphariya Khan or Zakkariya Khan, and in the profession box they had scribbled 'vagabond', and had added that this man's source of income was unknown. It is suspected that he earns his bread through pimping.

God is the sole bread provider, He is most resourceful, and He sees to final justice.

So, either a decade or two must have passed when Babbar Yaar Khan found himself, suddenly, an old man, a kind of old man of thirty, twenty-five years who had begun to lose hair and teeth, the one who could not face night without the help of intoxication. And the one who was going blind because of the growing syphilis.

During this period Babbar Yaar Khan, son of Zafar Yaar Khan, entertained the idea that the people who were responsible for axing him off the inheritance must be correct when saying that his deceased mother, Farrukh Zamani Begum alias middle daughter-in-law alias Jumrat, could not have been married, in the eyes of the law of the time, to his father because time's steamroller would not whistle away so slowly on top of him. That's why he somehow managed to reach the middle of the city and to Ayzad Yaar Khan's mansion, and took a dump right in front of the mansion's giant gate where the children of his uncles got off the cars; then without washing his arse, he returned satisfied. What else could he do anyway?

Have fun, fun, and more fun, bastard puppy!

A few decades are of such nature that neither Babbar Yaar Khan nor the city-dwellers know anything about. Only the spotted

Dullichan might know a bit here and a bit there. He too might not have come to know of it if it were not for the vicious stormy rain that blew away his tattered roof at night. Striking the staff on the road, carrying the dalda tin canister after the wind took away the roof, he reached the shed by the well with stairs. He would have never ventured to the shed if the street had not collected water knee-deep. If he could see the street, he would have made it straight to the Kirwani temple. Not that he was entertaining the idea of entering the temple; the fat temple-keeper would not have let him in anyway. In order to seek shelter at that time, what Dullichan could have done at the most was to reach the compound of the temple, raise himself up on four bricks on top of each other, and with the help of his staff hop across like a monkey to the raised platform, and then crawling along the platform go and lie under a vault and stay there contentedly in dry space till the rain abated. Everyone knew the vault and the technique, but Dullichan always found the spot empty. True, no one wanted to risk their life by lying there.

Whatever, Dullichan had reached the shelter by the well and now, leaning against the marble screen, he watched the dead souls of the Muslims emerging from dilapidated graves and splashing through rain water. Dullichan was not afraid of the dead. He was not much afraid of the living either, since the living beings were instead afraid of him. They kept him at bay. In fact, Dullichan suffered from a skin disease. The skin around his fingers, lips and eyelids had all turned white. The skin disease had also left white spots all over his face; the same was true of his neck and chest. People had whipped up the story that he suffered from leprosy; and that is why all the Muslims and Hindus, rich and poor, tried to get away from him and gave alms from a distance in order to save them trouble. That is how the skin disease saved Dullichan a lot of precious time; he did not have to spend much energy begging. On the other hand, it was unfair of people to have attached such an ugly disease to his name. He had no one his own who would show distaste at that unfairness,

Asad   Mohammad   Khan

and Dullichan's little heart did not even have the department that feels bad. That is why everything passed contentedly. If he wanted, he could have displayed anger, even cussed, but it comes down to a person's temperament; Dullichan did not want to upset anyone. He looked to the filthy weather now flatteringly with a smile on his face. He had no intention of making the weather worse by complaining.

Suddenly lightning struck and Dullichan saw a dead body of a Muslim headed towards the well, staggering, swaying, splashing water. Reaching the marble screen, he cussed Dullichan lakhera's mother, then tried to shoo him away by waving his hands. Dullichan did not mind it at all. He began to leave, but he noticed the dead Muslim had begun trembling seriously, later collapsing to the cracked floor, and died again.

Dullichan felt him afterwards; he had not died yet, only trembling because of cold. Either without thinking, or by way of flattering, Dullichan spread his own tattered blanket over the other body. But soon he began to regret, since the breeze carried the cold bite in it still. 'Whatever may happen now,' thought Dullichan, 'Whatever. At least he won't utter rubbish any more; he will let me sit with peace finally.'

Next morning when Babbar Yaar Khan opened his eyes, he as usual found himself in his grand-daddy's garden, where the spread of many thousand graves had been shrunk because the intoxication from the night before had not been broken yet. So Babbar Yaar Khan began thinking, sitting under the shelter by the well, wearing a new woollen shawl, about the night rains, wet and fragrant intimate rooms and child-widows. Without warning, a dark-skinned, ugly-looking man with white lips leaned over him to ask, 'What caste are you, brother?' Shit! All is spoiled. The woollen shawl, the shelter and Nawab Asfandyaar Khan's well and the garden (which he had inherited from his father) and the garden stroll with the child-brides in the rains of the departing winter, all was spoiled. A vulgar bolt of lightning has spread a landscape of graves in their place. Where did this white-lipped bastard pop up from? Babbar Yaar Khan held his head in his hands. He asked again, 'What cast are you, brother?' Babbar Yaar Khan weighed the question a while, then offered, 'Squatter, I am.' 'What kind, brother? Hindu or Muslim?' 'Neither . . . a bastard puppy only . . . Who are you?' The man with the skin disease replied with a tinge of flattery, 'I am Dullichan lakhera, master . . . This blanket is mine.' Babbar Yaar Khan could not control his laughter. 'Lakhera? A man worth a million? . . . ruined to dust? You too . . . eh?' Dullichan understood some and did not understand the rest but began giggling hehehehehe.

Both ugly-faced men began laughing.

God, or whoever created the world, must have created it while laughing and in love, because things cannot be created in anger, chaos, or detachment or boredom, because detachment and boredom are death's friends and anger and chaos are the children of defectedness and their colour is black and pale and their colour is white as camphor and this whiteness is different from the one that appears on the large jasmine flower, because jasmine is the colour of a laughter's flower, is the colour of God and when God appears in light and happiness, things are created, and whenever God creates things He laughs in extreme joy.

The scene of a skin-diseased man laughing remained stilled for a long time for Babbar Yaar Khan.

The scattered roof over Dullichan's head never came together again. He moved to the graveyard's shelter. Babbar Yaar Khan had taken to his flattering, his addressing him as master with his toothless mouth, and the choking laugh. Under the influence of receding intoxication, he considered the fact he was in the possession of the inherited part of the garden, poised on his own property (have fun and more fun, you fucking Landlord) and so this skin-diseased person is my servant, is my farmer, my attendant. 'Hey, master.' He told Dullichan to not waste his time wondering about the hut. There is plenty of space around the well. 'Hey, master.' We can both manage to hold on to a corner each. 'Hey, master.'

Asad Mohammad Khan

Dullichan brought back his canister, a metal pot, and his cup and saucer from the debris of the hut. This made up his entire world. From the moment of his arriving, he swept the shelter and, carrying water from the well in the canister, washed the cracked stone floor. Babbar Yaar Khan took two rupees out of his special pocket and sent Dullichan to the market to buy pakoras and both sat on graves to have their breakfast in the afternoon.

A few days later Dullichan collected a handful of bricks after wandering around the graves in the garden, built a round fence with them, and tossed dried leaves and twigs and dead skin of trees in it and started a fire there; then placed a canister of water on the bricks. After the water had been heated, he enticed Babbar Yaar Khan to wear his loin-cloth and asked him to come out of the shelter and there he poured water over Babbar with the dalda tin can. Babbar Yaar Khan cussed him while giggling and, searching with his hazy eyes, reached for his staff and tried to hit Dullichan half-heartedly, but lakhera stayed out of its reach. Staying at arm's length, he kept laughing his harmless and toothless laugh and pouring can after can of hot water.

Lakheras are magicians par excellence. People say lakh is the tear of the living trees; then they extract blooming, laughing rainbow out of those very tears; the par excellence magicians, those lakheras then extend the warmth of their own hands to the lakh, knead it in with the colours of sorrows and joys, toss it up in the air, draw it into circles, blow air on it to cool it down and then tie the tinkling rainbow festival around the wrists of laughing women. Lakheras are indeed magicians par excellence!

The one with black-yellow-coloured fingers, Dullichan too turned out to be a magician. The rascal showed fire to Babbar Yaar Khan, who too was a tear of a living tree, imparted him the heat of his hands and his shades of sorrows and joys, tossed him up in the air, drew him into circles and cooled him down with the blows from his mouth. Dullichan did not take him to the exhibition. He kept this singing, tinkling rainbow festival to himself. Because there arrives a day when the one who works

The Squatter

with his hands creates something which he does not bring to the market, but saves it for himself alone.

The free-loader had not made anything for himself in the last four decades. But what he made finally was quite something. While laughing with his white lips, he lifted Babbar Yaar Khan off a bamboo mat of the graveyard and leaned him against the marble screen. He cleaned the muck off Babbar Yaar Khan's eyes so the ill-fated could dream with clarity and more colours. And Dullichan pried open his breast, and in turn showed him his own wounds. He sobbed for him; made him sob too. Let him beat him; cussed him in turn; brought breakfast and drugs for him; then stole his money; committed thefts for him and then left him to his devices. But returned to see that the blind mother-fucker is clouded with flies hovering over his own filth. Lakhera kicked him mercilessly, wiped him clean with paper or wood or cloth, washed him with hot water and again made him sit against the marble screen. The city proceeded with its own speed. No one . . . not a single soul lifted a glance in the direction of the two ugly-looking men. Both were alive and prospering in the abandoned Muslim graveyard in the company of jackals, badgers, people who came here to get high and get laid and petty thieves. Babbar Yaar Khan used to address Dullichan as 'Dulli-da' which was a shorter way of addressing a big brother, or 'Lakhera-ji' or 'Lala', which no one else had ever done before. The music of those names and relationships rang in his black and yellow ears for hours. And when lakhera felt love for Babban Khan sahib, he called him 'Babbar Bhaiya' or 'master'. When angry, he would simply leave, but not without leaving enough water under the shelter and the Aligarh brand biscuits or pakoras and some liquor in a bottle. This was much better than what his father, clad in the silken jacket, had left for his Babbar Yaar Khan. He could reach the biscuits and liquor. That is why Babbar Yaar Khan was happy with him. He always used to pray for Dullichan for emptying the bottle. The words of the prayer were always that may God keep his man with the skin disease happy. Amen.

Those two discarded men could only live this way, in the company of each other till death claimed one of them because this way the two lived an absorbed life. The two wanted nothing more than this. But the city had turned over a new leaf.

(Around midnight the abdomen of the night was slit with a sound and a deadly river of white smoke began flowing over a crying, coughing, dying city. Over half a million inhabitants of the city began running on the shrieking streets of the blind city. Many thousands among them crumbled to the red earth of the city and, rubbing their heel on the ground, began dying.)

The incarnation of death, in the shape of fog, arrived at Asfandyaar Khan's garden as well and grabbed Babbar Yaar Khan and Dullichan by the throat.

The nearness of death made Babbar Yaar Khan's intoxicated state of mind clean and sober. The first thing that came to his alert mind was death was approaching without warning, so almost all the Muslims would certainly achieve martyrdom and by the grace of God all would enter Heaven of Firdaus. But the fear of death dominated the good news of unexpected martyrdom. Coughing, he tried to get up, could not, and began trembling. For another brief second a thought comforted him that when else a person of such bad character as he would get another chance of dying. Almost all the Muslims would achieve martyrdom . . . Dullichan lakhera could not comprehend this idea. First he made to run, ran out of the garden's boundary, but he left the blind to die behind. He felt a pang of guilty conscience and returned to the shelter by way of feeling the earth with his feet, and coughing. Mustering enough courage, he lifted Babbar Yaar Khan on to his back and once again came out of the garden. Facing was the whitish river growling and flowing on the cold street. Dullichan's sight was completely gone by now. When his lungs were about to burst, he deposited the sack of Babbar Yaar Khan on the government bench by the roadside. Coughing from weakness, the pile of bones first stretched open like a knife, then closed, and later fell off the bench. Dullichan considered for a minute

The Squatter {115}

that he must run away from here if he wanted to save his life, but everywhere he looked flowed the killing river of smoke which did not seem to have any limit. Dullichan fell on the empty bench and began waiting for Yamdut. He thought there was not much time left for the final call. So he recalled that he never was harsh on the weak; spent his life by making humble entreaties. 'I myself was weak, Prabhu. I did not even hurt the animals. Spent my life with two hands clasped humbly. So now let Yamdut's hand draw my life smoothly.' Then thought Dullichan so contentedly, 'I am indeed Karuna mai Grijapati's follower; am headed straight to paradise.' Beneath him Babbar Bhaiya began coughing terribly. 'But what will happen to this blind, since he is a Muslim?' How could Dullichan leave him here by the roadside after taking him out of the garden. Then he saw, in the river of milk, Yamraj's equipage and—heard the great thud of the massive bull. 'Hay, Parmeshwar! If this is the sign of Yamraj, then please take this Muslim in your protection too. Master, how is he going to find anything, this blind fellow in the darkness of the hell; show him the light, Prabhu!'

A frightening image moulded into thought appeared behind Babbar Yaar Khan's lifeless eyes as he lay beneath the strong bench made of cast iron and wood. The dead eyes saw a huge dark body and the dying ears heard the thump of heavy feet.

That was Yamraj, who had come to protect and take the wayfarer, the blind Babbar Bhaiya to heaven. He had certainly come on Dullichan's recommendation. ('There too we'll be an unbroken pair by the grace of God'. Thinking that, Dullichan's tiny spotted heart was filled with joy.)

'My God, keep my spotty man, this rascal happy. Amen.'

Right at that moment, below the bench, Babbar Yaar Khan prayed for Dullichan that O Merciful, this man has done many nice things for me. He has not yet breathed his last. Bless him, Make him a Muslim. How would he find his way alone in hell; he is alone, the rascal.

A s a d   M o h a m m a d   K h a n

So the Merciful accepted his good word and Babbar Yaar Khan heard, though with his failing hearing, the words of the kalma-e shahadat with surprising clarity. He heard that someone was rubbing his heels on the bench, reciting with a toothless mouth that I bear witness that I bear witness that I bear witness . . .

In gratitude, tears emerged from Babbar Yaar Khan's dead eyes. 'O God, you have showered the blessings of Islam on a heretic when no time was left. I give my life to your kindness, O God.'

Then, as he lay below the bench made of cast iron and wood, Babbar Yaar Khan son of Zafar Yaar Khan stretched his legs contentedly and died.

Two squatters, the free-loaders, were trying to enter the eternal garden of God in the company of each other while coughing.

—Translated from the Urdu
by Moazzam Sheikh and Elizabeth Bell

the tie that binds

Faiza Rana

The sun had not yet set when Father emerged from the men's quarters and walked over to the village square, where I sat on an old log on a side watching the rowdy boys kick up a duststorm that mushroomed skyward. The commotion the boys raised might even have woken God up. Still, my mind was somewhere else, as I seemed to be lost in the midst of the clouds, turning the colour of the sky paler by degrees. And I didn't even realize when Father placed his hand on my scrawny shoulder. Soon we were both walking on the deserted path, surrounded by wild grass and acacia trees, leading to the graveyard

I turned to look at the houses in the village we were leaving behind. In the middle, leading to the rooftop, were the rising walls with latticework, which had snared the sun as it seemed to emit long and hot sighs. I felt a shiver run down my spine and my hand, of its own volition, rose to my nose, where I still felt the dust, mingled with the feeling of irritation like kohl in one's eyes.

'Mithoo, what is keeping you?' Father used the name reserved for addressing me affectionately. I rushed to catch up with him. 'Child, you are young, but old enough to understand what I am about to tell you.' He'd been walking with his arm wrapped around my shoulder, but now he pressed me gently against him.

Originally published as 'Saanjh' in *Pancham*, June-July, 2002, Lahore

I knew he wanted to share something important with me. I too hid something important inside me, something that stirred like dust touched by a gentle breeze, then the next moment blew like a tortuous storm. But how could I tell him this! My mind caught hold of the thread tied to the storm and travelled backwards. The thread was long and studded with knots, descending into the past. As I pulled at it, a knot seemed to get caught in something, not budging to move.

A steady stream of tears fell from my eyes, yet Father pretended not to notice. He sat buried in the sofa, his lips curled tightly around the pipe of the hookah, smoking. My mother continued with her tirade: 'This too is unacceptable! You can't take it upon yourself to educate everyone's children. Remember, how you got *your* education? You paid your way by tutoring others. You used to have just a single pair of trousers and that too patched up. If it were due to your elder brother, then your younger brother would have been educated too. A good thing he could at least plough the land. The elder one still hasn't had his fill of idleness. And if the houses and shops in the city didn't bring in some income, they would be out on a limb—and they don't even own those completely. Now, you are an officer, by the grace of God. We don't lack in anything. They should keep their sons with them. It should be their headache whether they educate them or not. We have only one son. And his cousins pester him no end, forever stealing and snatching what he has. If I complain, you refuse to listen; I don't even exist. Go, ask your son, he is right here. Don't you even see his cheeks, all bruised from being bitten?' And with this she broke down, crumpled to the floor, wailing softly.

My father could take it no longer and, losing his temper, shouted her out of the room. As for me, he told me to go outside and play. I could feel the knots being tied once again, slowly, silently. Yet today a knot was coming loose with the force of a sudden storm.

On the deserted path leading to the graveyard, the shadows of the surrounding acacias were spreading. Caught in the latticework, the sun had breathed its last, and I had no idea how Father had been talking away. 'Mithoo, relationships are a blessing. You don't understand now, but you will as you grow up. Your mother's head is full of marbles. These folks are not strangers; they are your brothers—your older and younger uncles' sons. They are your arms. And see how they love you! Your younger uncle's son, Saaji, in particular. Try to understand: we live in the city. I am a government officer. I cannot till and plough the land. Nor can I buy land in my own name. Once you are old enough, you can get the land ownership transferred in your name. But even then you're going to need them to look after your land? Saaji will bring the grain to the city for you, just like his father does now . . . So you just be friendly with them now and don't worry your head over anything.'

I felt Father's voice darkening and merging into the surrounding shadows. Tears began to pour from my eyes, like the narrow stream of waste water that flows out in the open, warm and quiet in the cold and dark village nights. I couldn't let out a sound. Soon, both of us were slowly retracing our steps back home.

That night, sleep refused to come and Saaji refused to get off my back. I tried as hard as I could but to no avail, since my older uncle's son, Maaji, had me pinned to the ground with his foot pressing down on the back of my neck. And my nose, rubbing against the floor, was getting flatter and flatter. Saaji slid down a bit from my upper to lower back, his grip tightening around my waist.

I just couldn't lie down in bed anymore. I yearned to head out on the same deserted path to the graveyard—to fill my aching being with the darkness flowing from the acacias and the sound of the crickets hiding in the grass and reeds.

All was quiet in the courtyard. I sneaked out of the room through one of the large windows and entered the men's quarters. I was almost at the main door opening to the outside when something made me freeze in my tracks.

{120}   *Faiza Rana*

It was Father, standing just outside the door. I leaned back against the wall, my breathing agitated just as it had been the afternoon when Saaji had perched atop my back.

'Not Saaji's father but Saaji—as though he suspects something . . . all right, well, I should be off now.'

Leaning against the wall, I returned to the courtyard.

A dog howled for a moment or two in the village square, then all was quiet. I had grown up suddenly, and I had understood.

—Translated from the Punjabi by Amna Ali

the homebound

Asif Farrukhi

Naked to the bone, the morning suddenly stood before me and I was still fumbling with the locks.

The routine of my day begins, from the moment I wake up, with opening of locks.

My eyes are wide awake at the appointed hour. I leave my bed, although the night has not fully drawn away yet.

These are the very locks I close as my last duty of the day after I have checked every window and door before going to bed.

These days I do not wait for night to fall before I lock the door that opens to the street. The first hint of darkness is enough.

In fact, silence arrives in my city long before darkness these days.

Naked from head to toe arrives the morning. I endeavour to cover it up with the newspaper. By midday, however, the newspaper has been shredded to bits; by evening, the morning collapses to the ground in some alley of the city as a bare, nameless corpse.

Sullied by the stains of brutality throughout the day.

And like a crazy, homeless hag, the night wanders the city, shrieking.

That is why I keep the door of my house locked. Lest the shrieking make me a sleepwalker.

Originally published as 'Ghar Ghusna' in *Shehr-e Majira*, Maktaba-e Danyal, 1995, Karachi

Night or day; why should I have to offer my body as a sacrifice to the mindless, senseless firing in the air. I still have to open the locks in the morning; have to keep an eye on the day's work.

Moreover, I wish to live another day.

That is how I spend my days now.

At dawn I get up and come out, open the locks on the gate and turn off lights one by one.

Often the day has not yet fully dawned. I stumble in the receding darkness as I emerge and run into the empty cane chairs whose edges catch my clothes, trying to rip them as they stretch—the chairs appear, in the plodding spread of sunrise, like inauspicious spirits in the garden.

Soon it will be bright. The day's work will begin. I come out to sit on one of these chairs to read the newspaper. There is still some time before breakfast.

The newspaper has already arrived.

Rolled up, with a rubber band around it.

I have admonished the newspaper-man so many times, yet he continues to toss the newspaper the same careless way.

I have to bend down and search for it underneath the car; or among the flowerpots. I always find it in one of those nooks, the newspaper rolled up, with the rubber band.

I bring it in just as it is.

In the meantime, they all arrive as well.

I quietly put it down on the big table. No one opens it. They all look towards it. All wonder.

Then one manages: 'Eleven.'

'Seven,' says another.

'Five,' adds yet another. Why so low, they look at him.

'Thirteen,' the next voice announces.

I have not said anything. I look at them all.

I reach for the newspaper. Patiently, I remove the rubber band. It rolls down.

Before I can open the newspaper, he stops me, placing his hand on mine.

'No cheating in the bet,' he says. 'And, five rupees per point.'

'Five rupees? How do we figure out points?' All look to him, all asking.

'Whatever comes to be the difference from the actual number, that many points . . .' He smiles. 'And the points will be subtracted.'

He removes his hand. I open the newspaper.

The headline stares at me: terror reigns in Karachi, leaves 13 dead . . .

'I won,' he exclaims. 'All of you owe me now.' Making his point, he walks off to have his tea.

There is still time for my tea. I start to read the full news.

'I won't pay,' I speak up without having read the full report. 'Two men were killed perhaps due to a family enmity. It says here that the car was attacked near the Old Numayesh and the victim was a gambler, who ran gambling joints . . . There must be something more to the story.'

'What difference does that make?' He does not accept it. 'You are splitting hairs because you do not want to accept defeat.'

The rest put down five rupee bills in front of him.

All believe I have lost the bet. 'It doesn't make any difference whether he was a gambler or not; our bet was regarding the number killed in the city,' he says as he collects the money.

Well, I have to account for the gambler too. I know I will have to pay; the bet, after all, was regarding the number killed in the city.

It could be anyone's death.

Any kind of death.

The blood will spill on to the street.

And once blood is spilled, it must be accounted for.

At the appointed hour I will have managed to come and sit before the phone. My next resting place.

I have already made the arrangement. If another call comes in while I am on the phone, I can put it on hold.

He waits. I finish the first conversation first; then take him on.

We talk about the same things today as well.

Asif Farrukhi

I ask after him sometimes and sometimes after the city.

'How are things?' In response, he too may mean either.

'Don't ask,' says he. 'My friend, our situation is not very different than that of a confused Punjabi bumpkin.'

Whose situation could that be, I can very well guess.

Still, to be on the safe side, I ask, 'What happened? Is everything all right?'

'When I was conversing with you on the phone yesterday, you said something; and only after I'd put the phone down, did I realize . . .'

'What did I say?' I ask him. Only God knows what I said that was so strange.

'I had told you that I was losing courage to even walk out of my house. And you had said that you felt the same way . . .'

'That is true. I think of leaving the house and cannot do it. I feel extremely nervous about going anywhere. What if the road is blocked! What if a commotion breaks out! What if people start running wildly and I haven't a clue . . . If you go by car, then they check the car every other stop; besides, there is always the fear of being robbed at gunpoint. If you take the bus, you face other kinds of problems. Just the day before yesterday, I set out towards McLeod Road, and I'd barely gone past Teen Hatti when a piece of rock came flying from somewhere and hit a person seated two rows ahead of me, breaking his glasses, bloodying his face . . .'

I'll say mine when he is done with his, I felt as though he were tolerating me only for that reason.

'Yes, that is what I said,' he repeats. 'One dare not step out of one's house anymore. You too had said something to the same effect. Then you added that you had no courage left after yesterday's episode. But I forgot to ask you what had happened yesterday.'

What had happened yesterday? I sink into thought.

'Yes, that is what you had said. How are your wife and children? Have you received any bad piece of news from Acchay uncle's? Is your car running fine? Any work-related problem?

Anyhow, you did not mention anything remotely close to these. So what happened yesterday?' he elaborates on his question.

Yesterday's incident? But what incident? I am unable to answer him right away.

'I felt a knot tightening in my head after I spoke to you on the phone. I didn't think it right to phone you right away, lest it worry you. Then afterwards I picked up yesterday's paper. Regarding the attack on the police van in which three constables were killed, have those bullets reached your home by any chance? Is that why you are worried?'

Yes, that incident did take place. Very much like the incidents occurring in the city every day. But when I have to, I do get out of the house. What did happen yesterday? I try hard to recall. Despite trying, I cannot. With an apology, I hang up the phone. 'In fact, I was not referring to any single definite event; rather what is happening every day; is it not enough to scare us, cower us, make us homebound? Even when someone comes to meet me here, I do not relax until he has reached home and phoned me of his safety . . . but I must have said something more out of habit yesterday. What happened yesterday was not any different from what happens normally.'

Memory brings strange forgotten things from the past. Even if I shut my eyes and lie down, the brain turns into a lane filled with loud noises, people running chaotically and dumbstruck . . . so many of them, waiting for such a long time and they all had arrived only God knows from what great distances . . .

'Grandfather's youngest brother was preparing a concoction by thrashing down arsenic to pulp. He had the prescription. He would have rolled in money if he had succeeded . . .' This incident heard from Father so many years ago enters my memory with such detail and clarity that it seems it might have happened yesterday. Also, there was no apparent reason for it to come rushing to my mind at this moment. The incident has no direct connection to my days and nights now, nor do I remember it in its entirety. 'Two cats showed up from somewhere fighting each

Asif Farrukhi

other and grand uncle's concentration was momentarily broken. Soon afterwards, he began spitting blood . . . '

The voice fades out. To be replaced by another one.

'We were quite young and he used to take us for a walk. 'Come, let us go to the Company Garden . . .' he'd said one evening. But we had other plans. We made an excuse, but he saw through us and said, 'You boys are real mischief makers . . .'

I want to include others in the recollection also. Perhaps that will help me understand why such unrelated memories keep coming to me these days. I want to relate this incident to others, but no one listens to me.

When I start, they all start chattering away. Even mother ignores what I say and pretends to be interested in an argument between Father and Farooq. Every evening, this chitter-chatter comes cascading down—like the firing in the city.

'People who think this is nothing but a factional rift in one party will cry one day holding their heads in their hands . . .' Farooq was saying.

'Secretly they have cooked up the plan. They are making an ass out of the public . . . It is all orchestrated . . . Everyone is involved in this conspiracy. From the outside, they issue statements, but deep inside, they are destroying the roots . . .'

'Why are you quiet, Zameer, my son?' Finally Mother has noticed me. 'Will you have some tea?' She asks me in such a way I refuse, and, satisfied, she continues talking.

'I can't tell you how I felt that day. Such terror had seized the city . . . when evening fell the streets grew silent and sitting at home we felt as if our blood had dried up . . . We didn't follow the news. Instead we watched Evening of the Helpless on TV. The same noha was being recited, '*Ghabraye gi Zainub . . .*' Weeping, I had a fit of hiccups, couldn't help thinking the ill-fated Karachi itself had become the Evening incarnate. The next morning was the tenth of Muharram. Cruelty would reach its zenith. Now is the hour of murder of the helpless innocents . . . I could not sleep. All night long the image of young Sakina embracing her father's corpse, while others—sisters and daughters—wailed, kept spinning before my eyes.'

'So when we recited the last salaam I thought the final hour had come . . .' Father was saying, 'If this sorrow drags itself into the next year, we may no longer be here. All is in God's hands now . . . My heart pounded all night after hearing the crackdown was about to begin. Now they won't kill selectively; they are going to clean out entire localities . . . People had been watching from the rooftops, sounding the prayer calls by turn . . .'

'A silent terror hovered over the city that evening. It seemed the city would drown in a sea of blood. Then, suddenly the calamity was over. Was it because the strike and the protest were called off?'

'Who knows, we only learned about it in the morning newspaper . . .'

'I understand neither the strikes, nor the postponements,' Mother said sharply. 'First, the shopkeepers were losing, now they are gaining. I had stocked the necessary food items. But nothing happened. I am really fed up! Let what may happen, happen once and for all. But this everyday wait, the guessing, the fear, how long can one endure the dying and living every day?'

'People took a sigh of relief after a long, long time.' Farooq was addressing her.

Father felt it important to disagree with him. 'People breathed a sigh of relief, but they are a bit too relaxed . . . After seeing people's faces, happy and natural, it seemed the other day that things had gone back to normal. But everything is still stuck exactly where it was. The circumstances can revert any time. This is just a pause to regain energy. Meaning, we'll march on after catching our breath.'

'That means the city will go on gasping and the people dying?' Farooq was not ready to agree to such blanket statements.

'Those who are dead are gone, but I think about the ones who remain behind . . .' Mother has arrived at some other place in her thoughts. 'The woman from across the street told me yesterday about the woman who works at her house. Her son was shot. He

Asif Farrukhi

had gone to buy meat. He saw the meat dangling at the butcher's shop, but there was no one in line to purchase it. Before he could turn around, the firing erupted, and he was trapped. The bullet got stuck in his spine. Now he is crippled below the waist, confined to his bed for the rest of his life. He has three little children, and is only twenty-six, twenty-seven himself . . . death is far better than such a life . . .'

I cannot bear to listen any more. Why should I pray for his death, and then pray for how many more?

I turn away from the wall. I am in the house.

I place the books and magazines to one side. The TV is not plugged in. Approaching the light switch, my hand pauses.

The darkness that wanders all day has filled my room.

I lie down on my bed and pull the sheet over my face.

I do not want to think anything. I do not want to feel anything.

I do not want anything.

There is a noise outside. Let it be. What is it to me? The sound of hurried footsteps; the sound of too many people running. Someone is following them.

And this ring . . . no, it is not the telephone but the doorbell perhaps.

Who could it be at this hour?

I do not want to find out.

This is the sound of bullets. Incessantly echoing throughout the street, this sound. They don't remove their hand after pressing the bell. Are they going to knock down the door? What kind of a sound is this? Someone has jumped into the house! Running off at close distance . . .

And those chasing him . . .?

The knocks on the door are gradually turning into strikes.

I have not responded to it.

I do not even move from my bed.

I do nothing and I feel it is the right thing.

—Translated from the Urdu by Moazzam Sheikh

The Homebound {129}

old men

Asadullah Ghazanfar

The doctor had advised Haji Usman to stay clear of sweets, give up smoking, watch his fat intake and walk regularly. Haji had faithfully followed these orders for eight months and was now feeling much better than the previous year.

Some days he would even walk for half an hour straight. Now that winter was nearly over and the air was becoming warmer, Haji was also trying to increase his walking distance. Mamoor Latif had told him, 'You are acting like a young man; I refuse to accompany you any longer.' Like Haji, Mamoor was also eighty-four years old. Their health problems, however, were very different. Mamoor had heart trouble while Haji suffered from diabetes.

One spring evening, as he set out on his daily walk, Haji was feeling pretty courageous and free. The weather was so beautiful that he was prompted to take off his jumper, fold up his sleeves and unbutton the top of his shirt. The light spring breeze encouraged him to take a different route, and explore the streets of the city. His wanderings eventually led him to the park situated in the centre of the city. For a great number of years Haji had only visited the park in the morning.

Originally published as 'Buzurg Tana' in *Dastanoon*, Winter Issue, 2002, Peshawar

Mamoor Latif had once told him that in the morning parks belonged to the old and in the evenings to the young. Haji had been amused by this comment and had always managed to abide by this unwritten rule. Today, however, it had somehow slipped his mind. At the entrance of the park, Haji's eyes fell upon a young woman sitting alone on a concrete bench. He began to study her face; she had a wide forehead, a small nose, thin lips and big eyes Above all, Haji was fascinated with the soft look of her skin—a blessing of her tender age As Haji passed her, he said to himself, 'Why shouldn't I look at a flower in bloom? I am not looking at her with bad intentions.' He smiled to himself, beaming at the poor excuse.

As soon as he had come a little distance away from her, Haji stopped. He took a moment to analyse what he was feeling. For some odd reason he could not get her out of his mind; his long walk had increased his blood pressure and left his brain overly active.

Suddenly he thought of a trick to get her attention. He turned around and found her looking back at him. Her eyes appeared even larger and brighter than before. Unfazed, he casually asked, 'What is the time?' While she lifted her hand, he focused on her wrist. She glanced at her watch and Haji was taken in by the raising of her eyebrow. When she looked at him again, Haji longed for the same movement in her brow.

She responded, 'Quarter to six.' As she spoke, he could feel her breath and caught the scent of her perfume. Haji began to thank her when, to his horror, he suddenly realized that the young woman must have noticed his watch.

Haji quickly turned away and walked towards the centre of the park. He sat down on a bench and moments later dozed off. After ten or fifteen minutes of peaceful rest, Haji opened his eyes once again and remembered the young woman. He walked quickly to the entrance of the park, but she was nowhere to be found. His heart yearned to see her again, as if it would be his last chance.

He wandered around the park, looking at each bench and behind every tree. He searched the narrow paths between the rose bushes. The fragrance of the flowers and grass was prevalent, yet the scent of her perfume was missing. With a great sense of disappointment, Haji left the park. On his way home he realized where he had gone wrong; he should have searched for the girl at the other entrance to the park. He remembered now that the park had two entrances, one at the north end and one at the south end. Overcome with fatigue and already halfway home, he allowed his desire to see her slowly slip from his mind.

For his evening prayers, Haji went to the local mosque. 'How come you are so happy? What's going on?' Mamoor Latif asked him. 'Don't ask, I am so tired,' he replied. Mamoor stared at him with questioning eyes. 'Come with me tomorrow and I'll definitely tell you why,' Haji added. Mamoor's eyes seemed to smile as he nodded his head. 'Don't worry, I won't take you for a walk; I will show you something which will take you back to your youth,' said Haji reassuringly. That night Haji listened to the news, as he usually did. Chinese scholars in northern China had found a herb, which if dried, boiled and taken, was considered the best treatment for diabetes. He sat up and listened carefully. This piece of information had aroused his interest greatly. Early the next morning, well before breakfast, he put on his glasses and began reading the newspaper. The story had been covered in the papers as well. Haji read the story twice, taking in every bit of information.

Later on in the day Mamoor Latif came to visit his friend. Haji immediately told him of the Chinese scholar's discovery. Mamoor then asked him about the other news. 'What news?' Haji responded. 'The one you were mentioning in the mosque last night,' Mamoor reminded him. Haji couldn't remember. In an effort to jog his friend's memory, Mamoor added, 'You were saying it was something which would remind me of my youth.'

A s a d u l l a h   G h a z a n f a r

Haji became silent, trying desperately to recall the previous day's events. Yet nothing came to mind. Mamoor once again murmured, 'You were saying it was a way to freshen the heart.' Haji could not remember a thing. The young woman had fled his mind just as youth had said farewell to his life. After a few moments Haji enquired, 'Don't you think China has progressed a lot?'

—Translated from the Pashto by Gulalai Ahad

the buffalo

Sorayya Khan

Noor was five when she began to paint her dreams.

In the early Islamabad morning, Sajida stood in front of the full-length mirror in the corner of her bedroom applying eyeliner and lipstick and watching Noor in the reflection. Had she been standing, Noor would have reached Sajida's thigh. Noor was losing some of her baby fat and although she would always be round, she appeared to have shed the extra bracelets around her knees and wrists. At five (and earlier than her brothers), she'd already lost baby teeth, the curved gaps quickly filled with bone white teeth too big for her mouth. Crouched over her drawing and her orange bucket of sharpened crayons and pencils, the angle of Noor's back reminded Sajida of her husband, Hussein. As much as Sajida once loved him, she thought it unjust that her daughter, forsaken by her father, should have any physical likeness to him at all.

Noor, focused as neither of her brothers ever seemed to be, drew quickly and deliberately, her hand slipping from her paper and marking the bedsheets. Before Sajida pinned her hair and sprayed her favourite cologne on her neck, Noor had covered the bed with pictures.

Sajida was more lenient with Noor than with her other two children. Not only because of Noor's condition (the names, the ever-changing diagnoses of her mental state irrelevant, Sajida believed, to her beloved, but different child), but because she'd learned that marks on bedsheets could be washed away, there was always more paper to be had, and certainly, the peace of mind gained from a few uninterrupted moments was worth whatever mischief Noor came up with to fill them.

Sajida collected the pictures strewn around Noor, hardly paying attention to what covered them.

'Dekho,' Noor demanded.

Without looking, Sajida murmured, 'Bee-uu-tee-ful.'

Attuned to lapses of insincerity more than any of her children, Noor made her demand again.

'Dekho,' she repeated until Sajida sat on the bed, her freshly ironed dupatta wrinkling under the weight.

'Show Ammi what you drew.'

Noor took the stack from Sajida's hands and shuffled them. The first thing Sajida noticed was that all the pictures, except for a few scribbles here and there, were identical. It wasn't, however, until Noor pointed to the sharply outlined shape which curved at each end and inquired 'What is this?' that Sajida suddenly recognized the shape. It was the staple of a previous life she'd lived on the edge of a sea, a different country now, miles away.

'I don't know,' Sajida said, keeping what she saw, the boat, to herself. 'What did you mean to draw?'

'Noor is not mean,' Noor said, alarmed.

'Of course not. What did you want to draw?'

'Don't call names in the house,' Noor answered, mimicking Sajida's frequent reprimands to her sons, unable to let go of the insult she suspected her mother of directing towards her.

'This is . . . fish in a boat,' Noor finally said, intentionally smudging one of the surprisingly clean drawings with her fingertips. 'Fishboat.'

Sajida took the drawings from Noor and saw that she was right. Sajida finally recognized her daughter's word, *fishboat*, as a word she'd heard used many, many years before in a different language—Bengali—which she'd long since lost. In this other life, Sajida's younger brother or sister (she could no longer remember which) had used it to describe the boat her father and uncles used in their daily work to bring home fish from the Bay of Bengal.

Sajida reached for a pencil and printed *fishboat* in the corner of Noor's drawing. It was a habit that began months earlier when Sajida imagined she might teach her child to write by assigning one word captions to Noor's drawings. Noor wasn't much interested in shaping letters or even identifying them yet, but she enjoyed the certainty of Sajida's block-print captions. Sajida wrote slowly and meticulously, each letter the same size as the one which preceded it. She felt a vague sense of anticipation, as if with the unexpected familiarity of a memory that wasn't her own, Noor was launching mother and daughter on a journey yet to be named.

Sajida hung Noor's drawing in its place on a courtyard wall which Ali, Sajida's father, liked to refer to as Noor's Gallery. It was a growing, alphabetized collection of her drawings taped on to bricks and left to bake in the brilliant cycle of the Islamabad sun. Over the next few weeks, Noor drew the same fishboat scene over and over again, sometimes a dozen times in one day, until it was filled with great detail.

Then one night Noor had a dream of a tree with two fingers that rose into the heavens, a boat drenched in silver nets perched in the shadowed crook in between. Upon waking, Noor rushed from her bed into the bathtub. While others in the house slept, she scrubbed and scrubbed her feet again, because the grains of sand between her toes tickled when she walked. She had difficulty reaching the foot of her stiff leg, the one caught and broken by a manual cement mixer still parked near the driveway months after their new house was completed. She tied two washcloths together, hooked them around her sole, and rubbed back and forth.

'It was a dream!' Sajida said when she awoke. But try as she might, she couldn't make her daughter understand that dreams, in all their magnificence, despite the taste of salt and texture of sliding sand, were not real.

'Hear it!' Noor answered, pretending to run into the ebb and flow of imaginary waves.

Sorayya Khan

An hour later, the boat in Noor's latest drawing was brimming with dead and rotting fish. Sajida stumbled on the drawing on her way to the kitchen. She missed a step and leaned into the wall, as if it was required to keep her upright. More astonishing than the exactness of Noor's rendering was the startling truth that Sajida was again staring at the dead, rotting fish in silver fishing nets she had seen as a child wound around a tree.

Finally, when Sajida could speak again, she asked Noor where she had taken the idea for the drawing. Noor's capacity for language lagged behind her age by some years. But her response was immediate.

'From my head, Ammi.' Pinching closed her nose, coating her voice with more of a nasal hum than was her habit, she added, 'Smell the fish?'

Sajida nodded.

'Dreams,' Sajida was explaining to Noor, 'They're pretend.'

Sajida was making it up as she went along, never having been required to explain the difference between life and dreams to her boys. They'd known about it from the beginning, a similar miracle to the ability to distinguish sounds of Land Rovers from taxis and minibuses.

'I like dreams,' Noor offered.

'Of course. Sometimes you can go places you wouldn't otherwise,' Sajida answered. 'Like the sea. I couldn't take you to the sea. But you went there in your dream!'

'Why you won't take me?'

'I don't like it.'

'Why?'

'Big. Loud. I like the ground better.'

'When you were a snake-girl, Ammi. On the tree. You scared?' Noor asked softly.

Because Sajida had been wrapped like a snake in the tree and was plastered with mud near rotting fish in torn nets, Sajida understood Noor's question. Staring at her daughter, she wondered why Noor had omitted this detail in her careful pictures.

In the gallery of pictures that hung from the walls of the house, there was no place to hang pictures such as these. Where would they go, anyway, Sajida wondered. With *m*s for memories? Or *p*s for past life?

'No,' Sajida lied softly, 'I wasn't scared.' But she felt a shade of fear when she lied, as if the past and present of her life were shifting course, and were—inexplicably—rushing towards each other.

When Noor was no longer a child, and the family's stories were woven into knots and tangles, Noor brought up the drawing of the cyclone, her omission of Sajida in a tree.

'Didn't want to. Draw you scared,' she said, as if she'd known the truth all along. 'You're my Mama.'

***

It was Noor who brought the cyclone back for Sajida. Sajida, then, was the same age as Noor. She lived within walking distance of a sea full of fish on a shore of what was once East Pakistan but had since become Bangladesh.

All except Sajida's father had slept deeply that night. Before the cyclone, he was riding the sea in his boat. He prayed for a large enough catch in the dangling fishing nets so that when the sun rose again he might have earned respite from the water. Miles away, in a tiny village a few minutes walk from the coast, Sajida, her mother, and her five brothers and sisters were put to sleep after dinner by the soft patter of rain on their matted rooftop. In between their bedrolls, puddles sprang like islands from the carefully swept ground. In the land of East Pakistan, as much water as earth, Sajida liked to climb the only hill and watch the water recede. The young child knew the places her father's fishing boat could reach when waters were high: the paved road in the distance, the bicycle shop where rickshaws, bicycles and car tires were patched, and beyond, the low-lying bridge swept away with the rain of the season.

Sorayya Khan

By the time her mother awoke, the new baby already in her arms, it was not possible to distinguish the sound of the wind from the noise of the sea. Astonished, as always, at how soundly her children slept, her feet searched the ground for her plastic sandals. She found her voice and startled her children awake with her shouts. With one hand, she reached for her black sewing machine and when she set it on the small wooden crate, the only furniture in her home, the wheel next to the faded gold letters that spelled S-i-n-g-e-r spun back and forth like it did when one of her children played with it.

No one thought to run. Their lives were conditioned by the force and speed of water on their flat, flat land, and they knew they didn't stand a chance. Once out of their house, the children—including the thirteen-year-old boy who'd recently begun to resent looking at his mother when she spoke to him—tried to cling to her clothes. The smallest ones cried, frightened by the earthly roar that sent a constant thunderclap shiver into the ground they stood on. Her mother passed the lone acacia tree which in drier months blossomed in tight yellow flowers her girls threaded and braided into garlands. While others in the village scrambled on to the roofs of their feeble houses with the help of bamboo ladders and each other, she pulled her children towards the road in the distance where she knew a single metal pole was cemented into the ground. In a flash of lightning, she found the pole. Before instructing the older children to spread their arms around the pole, she kneeled down to secure the younger children and gave Sajida the baby, warning her, Sajida would for ever remember, to be careful.

After the worst of the water had receded, when Sajida was found alone, her body and clothes torn and battered by the fury of the sea, no one knew how long she had been there. She did not make a sound when the relief workers approached.

In striking distance, their legs knee deep in the mud and water that ravaged the roots of the only two trees to be seen for miles, it was not any easier for them to trust what their eyes revealed.

The Buffalo

An old, splintered tree with a trunk no wider than one of the men's waists, held, in the fork of its twisted branches, an unscathed fishing boat. The name, printed in black and in English, graced the sides: the *Freedom* bold and deliberate, as if it had been painted in oils the previous day. The tree carried the boat like a trophy, thrusting it into the sky as if each inch of branch had grown for this purpose alone. It was after the men accepted what they saw that the stench became overwhelming. The boats' silver fishing nets, filled with rotten fish the colour of brown bleeding into black, hung from the tall tree. The nets shimmered in the gleam of the sun like a lace curtain.

Two pink men made white by the sun. By the time Sajida saw the men coming from her tearing eyes, she'd been hugging the tree with her body for so long it seemed to be doing it on its own. It was only because her body had joined the tree that they had such difficulty extracting her. She wanted to help, to make a sound, but her limbs, like her throat, refused.

One of the men touched her. The girl's skin, nothing like bark, gave way like that of fresh corpses he had lifted, carried, and set aside. The girl's body was wrapped around the branch as tightly as a snake's, and when they found her head by the trunk, facing the sky, they did not expect to find life. But the soft, weak breaths drawn between her swollen lips and tongue suggested otherwise. The two men, first flabbergasted by the reminder of life in one tree, and now by the existence of it in the other, used all their strength to pry loose the girl. They took turns carrying her, a meagre child whose ankle bones and wrist bones jutted from sores on her body as if her insides were spilling out.

As they carried her to dry land, her head near one of their armpits and then another, Sajida smelled their skin, traces of unfamiliar soap and sweat made sweet because of it. With mud in their boots and an almost dead girl in their arms, the two men somehow managed to find land that did not sink underneath their feet.

In the relief camp, piled with blankets, her body shook all night. In her nightmares, she heard her mother's voice rising

S o r a y y a   K h a n

from the bottom of the sea. At first her mother had spoken the simplest and most common of daily reminders: *wipe the hair from your eyes, take your thumb from your mouth, take the laundry bundle to the river.* After a few nights, Sajida was addressed like an adult in her communications with her dead mother. *You make shalwars,* Sajida was told, in anticipation of the place in which she would spend the rest of her life, *by cutting the cloth in two arms' lengths, exaggerating the width of the man's legs, and sewing the seams on the inside before stitching the cuff's border for decoration.* Sajida was tempted to believe that her days were dreams and her nights, spent in the company of her mother's clear voice, were not.

***

Noor squeezed her last *fishboat* on the wall, in between *fan* and *farmer.* The difference with this drawing was that when Noor passed it, she held her nose as if her fishboat brought its stench into the courtyard of her grandfather's house.

Some days later, Sajida awoke to a picture on her pillowcase. She saw an animal, *a buffalo?*, grotesquely bloated, his head that of a different, more kindly beast. As in Noor's very first pictures, every inch of the paper was covered with colour. This time it was brown, exactly the right brown-black of the mud after the cyclone, and the buffalo sank in it. Sitting up, Sajida lifted Noor's work from the pillowcase. In Noor's drawing, Sajida saw a young girl, clothes ripped from her, clumps of hair plastered to her forehead and her neck. Her small hand disappeared into the buffalo's monstrous body. In the corner of the drawing, there was an outline of a baby. *The longest of lashes*, Sajida noted, eyes drawn perfectly closed. The recognition of this detail more than any other made Sajida's hands go cold.

When Sajida had her boys, she would sometimes hold on to them for *dear life!* (as Hussein would say), overwhelmed by the memory of the baby Noor had just drawn. After their bodies outgrew their need for her, she'd find the boys in the courtyard or sitting at the table doing their homework and wrap her arms around them and squeeze as if her life depended on it.

Sajida's mother had handed Sajida her baby brother. There were so many children, and only one pole. Then the sea was before them, in a wall so high Sajida could not tell the bottom from the top. Light, all of it, lanterns, flashlights, candles, fires, lightning, vanished and the blackness was a hole of dizziness and terror. The wave lifted Sajida from her feet more easily than her father could sweep his children into his arms. The pole slipped from her grasp as if it had never been there, but she held first the baby and then her breath, the way she'd learned from her eldest brother when they'd jumped in water to keep them cool. She was thrown so high, so far, so deep, the baby wrenched from her arms. Flailing, her hands struck something solid. She dug into the hardness while her body, desperate for air, was swallowed into a sea. When she awoke she was holding on to a dead buffalo. Swollen, floating like a boat.

Except for the baby, Sajida's recollections were scattered.

Her mother's last *Bismillah*. Broken into pieces and thrown back by a wall of water. *Freedom*. Her eyes trained on the sea for the shape of her father's boat, his silhouette at the edge of it. The camp, old men, voices without strength or inflection. Imagining bits of her mother floating through dark valleys near the ocean floor, scraping rocks and shells in the pit of the sea's belly where sound, like light, did not reach. Dreams filled with demons and gods who were equally cruel. Later (*but how much later?*), keeping herself steady, one palm flat in the air, the other on her knee, as a makeshift chair of a man's arms lifted her from one place to another.

Sajida didn't remember all the details, the rhythm of the story, how it ran one way and then another and then back again, like water rushing about. Hearing her daughter scratch on her drawing tablet on the other side of the room, Sajida blinked and studied the drawing: the eyelashes, long and curled as she was certain they had been. Noor, she thought, this child, so sweet and magical, born not of this world, but of another.

* * *

For years, Sajida and Noor slept together in Sajida's marriage bed, a king-size bed the family carpenter built for her. It had a high backboard with several panels of woodwork, rows of intricately carved flower buds that blossomed from one panel to the next. She'd gone to the bazaar by herself to order the bed. The carpenter gave her a cup of tea, and while she sipped the sugary mixture, he sketched examples for her on the faded newsprint of old dailies. She wasn't keen on big furniture, but it seemed natural to her that her marriage bed be an exception. She toyed with the idea of posts and canopies, footboards and odd, pull-out night tables she'd seen in a home decorating magazine. Then the carpenter transformed a thick piece of wood with his chisel into a lily before her very eyes. She lifted it from the carpenter's hands and held it near her nose, half expecting it to exude the fresh, after-the-rain smell she loved so much.

When Hussein moved out of her bed (and their life) on to a mattress in another room, she stopped thinking of her bed in the same way. The flowers were simply the headboard against which she lay while she nursed and rocked her daughter to sleep. Later, when Noor no longer required her embrace to sleep, the headboard, useless, was virtually forgotten. But Sajida became increasingly mindful of the parameters of the bed and she wondered how a bed that was large, even for two adults, could be so cramped. Her nights were interrupted by Noor's restless dreams in which the child travelled from the foot of the bed back up and from one side to the other without regard for the presence of her mother. Often, Sajida's side was bruised where Noor's legs, the strong and weak one, left their marks on her.

But the day after Noor left a drawing on Sajida's pillow, and through what Sajida could only attribute as a miracle, Noor was overcome with a newfound and urgent need for privacy.

'Noor ka bistar,' Noor said one morning, pointing at Sajida's marriage bed and making it her own. 'Where is Ammi's bed?' she continued, holding her hands up, as if another bed, her mother's, might suddenly appear like an apparition at the heels of a suggestion.

It took Sajida a moment to respond, unprepared that after all these years she was being released by her daughter, if only for a few hours each night.

'I'll fetch another bed,' she finally said, gently lowering Noor's hands to her side. 'Ammi's bistar is coming.'

Sajida did not think twice about relinquishing her bed. She poked her head in the storerooms near the servants' quarters, and in the second one retrieved a single bed. The cot was nothing but woven jute loosely strung from a simple frame, but Sajida was not interested in the specifics. The servants forced the bed behind a divider of faded velvet curtains into the tight space of the dressing room, a narrow, dark alcove of sorts that had never been put to proper use. Sajida took to the itchy cot in the claustrophobic room, as Hussein might have said had he been speaking to her, like a fish to water. Sajida loved her child, utterly and completely, but the fact was that Noor had encroached on her nights even before she was born.

Alone, Sajida slept more deeply than ever, night after night surrendering to a deep slumber filled with dreams that had beginnings and endings. She no longer rose with the light of the day as she had her whole life, even when her children were infants and her nights were exhausting hours of rocking and feeding. Instead, Sajida slept through dawn in the darkness of her alcove. Sometimes, she was awakened by Noor. Noor would draw open the discoloured curtains in an impatient rush and the clatter of the metal rings running over the rusting curtain rod delivered Sajida into the next day.

Once in a while, with streaming sunlight behind Noor, the sight of her dishevelled daughter in a rumpled dress she'd refused to exchange for nightclothes before bed made Noor appear more a vision than a child. On those mornings, Sajida marvelled at the God who'd made this special child her own.

***

Ali, Noor's grandfather, came across Noor's drawing while he was tidying some newspapers in the lounge. It was caught between the morning and afternoon dailies, a burst of energy tucked in black newsprint. On principle, Ali liked anything Noor drew, although he was partial to the foods she managed to illustrate so exactly he sometimes found himself with an appetite after looking at them. A few years earlier, when Noor's drawing talent surfaced, Ali drove to the marble factory at the edge of Islamabad and purchased the finest piece of marble he could find. Workers placed the flat stone in the courtyard early one evening. From that time forward, Noor mixed colours into drawings perched on the polished white stone.

The drawing Ali held in his hands was slightly different from what Noor usually drew. It was lacking a caption from Sajida: no *storm* or *rain* or any other description. More importantly, the brown-black of the background, the images of torn, upside down trees and beaten boats, were drawn from an odd perspective, as if from above rather than inside the scene. Yet there was a special mist of grey that ran across the picture—so certainly, Ali knew at first glance, that of East Pakistan's monsoons. The contradiction that struck Ali was that one had to be *inside* the rain, feel it beat down steadily to know the colour, the length of the sheets. Nothing less would do. He knew this unequivocally. Now, whenever the monsoons arrived, planting a roar inside his head, he lay awake in his bed recalling the symmetry of falling sheets of rain, the pounding of the drops, and the sinking mud.

Ali thought of the last monsoon season in Islamabad and remembered, with a start, how he and Noor had stood one suffocatingly hot day in the middle of the courtyard when the skies emptied with rain and steam rose like smoke from the fine

The Buffalo　　　{145}

marble slab and the red bricks of the house. The two of them danced and slipped on the drowning marble, celebrating like poor, unclothed children in the alleys of a Rawalpindi bazaar before Sajida put a stop to their fun.

Was it grey like that? Ali tried to recall, suddenly able to smell the mud and rain, months later, on a day in April when the sky held nothing but a brilliant sun.

The drawing stayed with Ali, and he finally understood where it belonged: with the *c*s for *cyclone*. Late at night, lying in bed with a sheet pulled to his chin, hands next to his sides, palms flat, ready, as had been his habit in the army, he recalled what he'd seen.

From above, in the airplane, there was no question. East Pakistan was beautiful. Lush and green the way West Pakistan never was, even during the monsoons. Snaking rivers and endless tributaries flowing like life itself through the rich fields. The earth so fertile it hardly needed seeds. The land is black like the people, *someone had said,* only not as lazy.

The flight lasted hours. It circled around the tip of India and when the plane couldn't land in Dhaka because of the fighting, back down again to wait in Sri Lanka. Twenty-one hours later, again morning, it landed. Dried mud was preserved in the most unlikely of places—tops of trees, airplane hangars, tin roofs of the barracks. Who hadn't heard about the cyclone? East Pakistan, *it was said,* always and forever unlucky in the mouth of the Bay of Bengal.

By the time I got there, the bloated buffaloes had long since fed the crows and the flies. Carcasses crumbled across the land. The air was heavy, but not with rain. Everything, living or not, seemed alive with hate. The roads, the trees, the bicycles, the bharis. The first night, walking the streets of Dhaka looking for miscreants, I scarcely dared to breathe. Within hours, I was gulping at the air greedily, as if, already then, to prove I was still alive.

S o r a y y a   K h a n

Come back home, *Auntie had said. But right then, it was so far away, it might have been another world. If it existed at all.*

Did you know that?

Sitting in his armchair, glancing at the newspaper headlines, Ali heard Noor dragging her bucket of supplies across the brick path in the courtyard. Along with the slight limp of her once broken leg, keeping her bare, flat feet inside the rectangles of the bricks, never on the lines, resulted in slow going. Some minutes later, she presented herself in front of Ali in a freshly starched dress for her morning embrace while the cook readied her plate. Noor was in a cucumber stage, and for the second time that day, the cook had scraped out the seeds and carved what remained into identically sized triangles. The cyclone lay on the cocktail table, next to the cucumbers.

'See?' Noor asked, picking it up.

'My artist,' Ali said, and although sitting, he attempted a waist bow. Noor squealed with delight.

'Bow to the Queen!' she exclaimed, standing, the ruffles on her frock suddenly appearing regal.

'Kya?' Ali said, asking Noor to identify the animal she'd drawn.

'Buffalo,' Noor said. 'Fat.'

'Fat, indeed!' Ali said.

Noor picked up the salt shaker. She unscrewed the cap, took out a pinch of salt, and sprinkled it on the tens of tiny triangles on her plate.

'You've seen a buffalo?' Noor asked.

Ali studied the drawing, looking beyond the mist. He looked at it from different angles, tilting the paper this way and that, examining the animal, eyes bulging, *gone maybe*, the head small compared to the immense belly. *Fat and stiff. Dead.*

Startled at the facts of the drawing, he looked from the buffalo to his granddaughter.

'You've seen a buffalo like this?' Noor asked again.

He let a few minutes pass.

'People like this,' Ali said so softly he wasn't sure Noor heard him above the crunch of her cucumbers.

hieroglyphics

Fahmida Riaz

Laila opened the window of the guest house of the beautiful university campus sprawled by the sea shores, and welcomed the first rays of the morning. She noticed the paper with her day's itinerary lying on the table. She was a traveller from far off. Distances, however, meant very little—this was the beginning of the twenty-first century, synonymous with the world shrinking not only due to the technological revolution in communication, but also because various travel facilities enabled people of every colour, nationality and religion, to go from one end of the earth to another, crossing mountains, forests and oceans. Yet, unending conflicts between followers of various creeds and religion, the increasing awareness of what is mine and what is yours, and the violent insistence on it, have filled these distances with tension.

Now searches at every step, questions, and heightened security welcome us at every airport. Although the fear of airplanes being hijacked, of bloody events in the airport or the aircraft, and smuggling in of weapons have turned it into a nerve-racking experience, countless people continue to journey, day and night, to far-off places. The distances covered by road or sea in the past are now covered on the wings of air. With the increase in population the number of world travellers has also increased; reasons for travelling haven't changed for thousands of years, however.

Originally published as 'Khat-e-Marmooz' in *Aaj*, Summer/Fall issue, 1998, Karachi

So, Laila, a woman writer from the East, too, had travelled from one end of the earth to another

She had arrived in the US on the invitation of several universities, fully aware that these universities were rich enough to spend on the travel of any number of people, from any corner of the world.

Laila had accepted the invitations from the universities with joy and gratitude, and in keeping with the centuries-old tradition of writers and artists, had undertaken this journey in the hope of some pleasure, combined with learning and broadening her outlook. In her eastern clothes, carrying a small travel bag on her back, she had passed through many airports and distinctly felt the obvious disdain of western travellers and airport employees at her garments and eastern looks. Maybe these looks, she considered, were of admiration and curiosity. But, then, how could she be so judgemental when a few days before her departure, an excited mob had violently targeted some western women tourists only because of their western attire.

So she ascribed their insensitive looks of displeasure to bad manners and moved on. The frustration experienced at the airports faded at the university. Here Laila's time spent had been very useful and pleasant. She had lectured the students and discussed literature and learning with the teachers. She had been plied with delicious food and drink, and in every city had been taken to plays and concerts, museums and other places of entertainment. On these occasions students and scholars belonging to her region had been invited to keep her company. Most of them were Hindus from India and spoke her language, although their accents were slightly different. Enmity between Indians and Pakistanis had persisted for over half a century. Even writing letters across the border was fraught with danger. Here, in this land of strangers, scholarly and serene people embraced Laila with unbelievable warmth.

Laila's last lecture had been scheduled for that day; later she was to embark on her journey back home. She had packed and was ready at daybreak. She had also gone over her written speech and marked out the relevant portions in the reference books.

It must have been close to ten when her hostess, a well-dressed, young scholar from the Centre of Eastern Arts and Literature, arrived and took her to the building at the far end where the offices and classrooms of the Centre were located. On the way she informed Laila that since she had some time before her lecture it had been arranged for her to meet a literature Professor.

Laila entered the corridors of the building through glass doors that opened automatically. As she read the nameplate on the third door, she realized she was to spend time with a person of Jewish background.

The room was small enough to be called a shelter. Two of the walls were hidden by thick books and a layer of paper dust coated the room. Opposite the entrance there was a window with a wooden table placed just below it. The Professor sat bent over the table with his back to the door. When he turned around, Laila saw a glassy film covering his clothes and face. And when he welcomed Laila, the voice seemed to come from cracks in the glass.

'Thanks for coming by,' the Professor said. 'I am fortunate to have a woman writer from the East spend time with me.'

He was looking at Laila intently taking in her rust-coloured clothes with tiny mirrors stitched into the embroidered flowers and buds. She wore a gauzy stole, with a delicate lace border interwoven with gold thread, draped around her shoulders, exuding the fragrance of sandalwood. Laila bowed slightly in acceptance of his greetings and then hesitantly stretched her hand out. The Professor seemed confused about whether he should shake her hand or not. He appeared so taken aback by Laila's outstretched hand that she immediately withdrew it and looked around the room smiling pleasantly. He asked her to sit down.

There were two uncomfortable wooden chairs in the room. He took one and Laila sat down on the other. The Professor looked at her. Under his gaze the rust-coloured clothes and stole transformed into sensuous drapes, swaying, with the mirrors and

Fahmida Riaz

red and black silk embroidery. After an awkward silence the two attempted to converse.

Laila spoke first, 'I too am extremely fortunate to have got this chance to talk to you. But tell me, this is the Centre for Eastern Studies and you teach English literature. Why have you been given a room in this building?'

The Professor smiled, 'This is because for the past years I have been learning, and teaching Sanskrit.'

Laila smiled in surprise and her voice betrayed the fact that she was impressed, 'That is wonderful! I feel encouraged by it. For a while now I have been thinking of learning Arabic but get discouraged by the thought that new languages can only be learnt when one is young.' Then, a moment later, she added, 'Maybe if I tried I could learn. I can read Arabic though.'

The Professor's eyebrows went up questioningly. If this woman could read Arabic then where did the question of learning it arise?

Laila read his expression clearly and explained, 'Our holy book is in Arabic which all of us are taught as children. But, this does not teach us the language.'

The Professor nodded his head and Laila observed that his eyes were amber coloured and his ruffled hair was an earthy brown. The same glassy veil formed over his eyes and she noticed golden hair peeking out from under his upturned sleeves.

'Yes . . .' the Professor took a short cold breath and said, 'Arabic . . . I too would like to learn Arabic. And you . . . What is your language?'

'Urdu,' Laila replied. Then she thought a while and explained, 'This is almost the same language as that spoken by the people of northern India.'

'Well! Really!' he exclaimed in surprise. He had studied in India for several years, but was unaware of this fact.

'Yes!' Laila answered, 'But . . . their script is different.'

Laila's last sentence caused his face to light up. At the same instant, for some inexplicable reason, Laila observed that two or three buttons of his bluish shirt were open. It was also clear that for a long time no one had tried to remove the wrinkles in his clothes with a hot iron. Seen through the glassy film he appeared all wrinkled and creased. Laila looked at the golden hair protruding from under his rolled-up sleeves, but the Professor, oblivious of her gaze, was lost in his thoughts.

'Script . . . the script is very important.' It was clear that he had pondered on this subject for a long time. Then he added, 'The entire character of a nation or race is embodied in the script that it uses to write its language.'

Laila was startled at this pronouncement. Taken aback, she stared at his face.

The Professor noted with interest that all the flowers on her dress were now glowing like flames from a lamp.

Laila sighed, thinking. She asked, 'And what is the Hebrew script like?'

This time the Professor was startled, 'The Hebrew script . . .?' he repeated in surprise. Now suspicions began to take root in his heart, 'But you . . .', he said, 'Why are you taking an interest in Hebrew?'

Laila got up from her uncomfortable chair and went and stood by the table in front of the window. The white paper lying on the small wooden table was almost blank. There were two or three sentences scrawled across one corner but the writing was so fine that Laila could not read it. She was confused. She had not expected this question from him. Indeed even for her it was sudden and unexpected that she was interested in Hebrew. Often, she would not go into detail about why she was taking interest in a certain subject and so with some hesitation she replied, 'I do not know much about the evolution of the Semitic languages . . . I suspect that Arabic and Hebrew are evolved forms of each other.'

The Professor nodded his head with some disbelief. Laila expected him to ask why she was so interested in the fact that the Arabic and Hebrew scripts were similarly constructed. Laila was not a scholar. She was only a writer, whose mind's universe was like an intense powerful tide, expanding and contracting. She couldn't predict the direction of the tide. And this irritated her.

Fahmida Riaz

However, she spoke in an even, dignified tone, 'I am more interested in the social reasons than literary.'

He seemed to comprehend this somewhat though he was not willing to admit it. He pushed the chair nearer the table, then with a wooden ruler pointed to the corner of the blank white paper.

'This is the Hebrew script,' he said with a weak laugh. 'My daughter came to my room this morning and left this message for me.'

His daughter could read and write Hebrew. She had spent three years in Israel. This morning she had been in a hurry to go somewhere and had not had the time to go to the house where her divorced father had been living alone for the past ten years, with a faithful black dog. Black and white photographs of his family taken fifty years ago in some part of Europe, hung on the walls. The dust on these had not been cleaned for months.

Laila looked at the slanted writing on the corner of the paper and said, 'The writing is very fine. I cannot separate the words from each other. You write and show me.'

He wrote something in Hebrew on the paper and then read it aloud.

Laila stared at the writing with interest and curiosity. Then she said, 'Perhaps . . . my suspicion . . . is correct.'

'Meaning?' The Jewish Professor asked softly.

'These contours and sharp curves are similar to the Arabic script but . . . the placing of parts of the letters seem different . . . This "*saa*" that you have written has two curves like the "*seen*" in Arabic, but their positions are different.'

Laila made the large contours of '*seen*' on separate, small pieces of yellow post-its and changed the positions and showed it to the Professor. She was now standing beside him. When she bent down to write something on the paper she suddenly encountered a waft of sandalwood mixed with the smell of her own body. Laila was surprised. This was only possible in very hot weather. She had been brought up in the eastern land of Sindh. There, on dry, hot afternoons, she had smelt this fragrance often, emanating from her own body. She remembered with amazement that Sindhis called this odour '*saa*'.

'*Tamachi ji Saa,*' Laila whispered.

'What?' he asked in a heavy voice.

'I was speaking in the Sindhi language,' Laila replied.

Then she wrote a few lines in the wide Sindhi script on a piece of paper.

'What is this you have written?' he asked.

'Down below is water, up there the sky and on the side the winding path of the forest, In the middle the fragrance of Tamachi's body comes and goes,

The west wind blows

The Kinjheer lake lulls you like the cradle.'

'Very nice!' The Professor nodded. His handsome face was now suffused with happiness, eagerness and curiosity. He began to realize that the aroma of sandalwood mixed with the fragrance of this eastern woman's body which now engulfed him was very pleasant. He remembered the smell of sunflowers which grew in wild bushes in his backyard every spring, and whose chocolate-coloured spores were scattered by the wind.

'Is this . . . also the script of your language?'

'My language?' a discomfited Laila laid eyes on the word she had written. 'No . . . No . . .' She replied with a strange sadness, and from somewhere far off, very far off, the smell of burnt flesh singed by a cigarette assailed her.

'How will you write this word in your script?' He asked, pointing to a word.

'We write it like this . . .' Laila replied and wrote 'khinjeer' and hesitantly continued, 'but . . . the phonetics of these words cannot be rendered in the alphabet of Urdu.'

She fixed her gaze on the word 'khinjeer'. For an instant each curve of her writing seemed like a dagger dipped in blood. She quickly looked away. Now there was no sign of red on the white paper. The earth is so vast, she thought, and its diameter so large, so how could all this be explained to him?

Fahmida Riaz

She was standing behind the Professor as though in a trance. She saw that the brown hair at the back of his neck were turning grey. And the collar of his shirt was frayed. Suddenly she wanted to touch the frayed edges with her fingers.

The Professor stood up from his chair. The glassy film on his arms, face and clothes cracked loudly and the clear shards fell on the floor. He stood beside Laila. The tall woman came up to his chest. He quietly took in a deep breath of the warm fragrance of Laila's hair and delicately passed his hands over the Hebrew letters on the paper. On every curve of these letters he saw refuge his people could take. This was the refuge after generations of exile, refuge from the gas chambers, the sudden explosion of bombs, the scattered bloodstained body parts . . . how could this eastern woman understand this?

Laila sat down. She took the pen in her hands and before writing raised her head and said, 'That is the Nastaliq script which is Farsi . . . Persian . . .' Laila said the words 'farsi' with her teeth pressing on her lower lips, '. . . which perhaps earlier was Parsi.' She put her lips together to say 'parsi'.

'Parsi,' the Professor repeated. His lips came together and then parted.

Laila bent down over the paper and wrote words of her own language. While laying out the arches and lines she imagined the domes and minarets, masterpieces of architecture. This was a dignified, delicate, serene writing whose every letter seemed poised to touch the sky.

The Professor took the pen from her hands and wrote down some Hindi words on the paper. Laila stared at the curves of this writing, whose pleasant form pulled by some divine force seemed to leap towards the earth's navel. The words were like a blossoming vine with tender bell-like flowers among the dense leaves.

When both these scripts were put side by side their differences became clear.

The Professor's amber eyes were observing the scripts as well as Laila's face intently. Without doubt even a stranger could see how different these scripts were, so apart in temperament that it was not possible in any way or any form to bring them together.

Laila's eyes were taking in the words. Her face was thoughtful and confused. The light coming in through the windowpanes lay golden on the paper. Finally her confusion ended.

'This . . . this script . . .' she said softly, 'reflects the character of a race, the hopes of the past, present and future . . . but . . .' she said without any hesitation, 'look at this . . .'

Then with her pen she made the following patterns:

\# * ^ ~'< . . . .

He looked at these with great interest and then eagerly asked, 'Very nice! What script is this? Is this some ancient language of your region? These look like hieroglyphics in which the ancient Egyptian scrolls are written.'

Laila stood up straight and looked at the writing. There were stars twinkling in her eyes. In a trembling voice she replied, 'This is a secret code . . . a hidden cipher . . . I have invented this. I was thirteen or fourteen years old when I fell in love with a boy. We would use these symbols to write to each other so that if it fell into someone's hands they would not be able to read what it says.'

The Professor looked at her in amazement. Then he said, 'How interesting! Where are those letters?'

'Those letters?' Laila repeated, then recalled, 'in the courtyard of our house were two big pots with rose bushes in them. One night I dug up the earth and put in the letters . . . all the letters . . . in this pot with the rose bush.'

'But . . . what is written here?' He asked with curiosity.

'I love you,' Laila replied in a flat tone.

Stravinsky, the Jewish Professor, stared at her. Another glassy film crumbled. As she turned to leave the room he gently tugged at Laila's gauzy stole and it fell away from her body. The buttons of his own shirt opened easily. On the grey floor of this den,

Fahmida Riaz

experiencing the ruptures deep inside this strange woman from the East, he closed his eyes contentedly and it was then that he realized that he had accepted the meaning of a language which in spite of being very ancient was alive and well. All the racial, ethnic and religious bloodshed that had taken place till today had been unable to relegate it into a dead language.

About Laila's lecture, its time had passed long ago.

—Translated from the Urdu by Aquila Ismail

paths

Azra Waqar

When I visited Bangladesh twenty-seven years after its birth, I asked Daisy: There are photographs of your war of independence on display at the museum . . . Pakistani Army, corpses, dogs—what message do you want to convey to your younger generation?

We have preserved history, she said.

You have *changed* it. You have deformed history.

How so?

As we came across a book titled *Our War of Independence: 1947–71* at a bookstore, Daisy lowered her eyes. When Army Action took place in Bangladesh, I hid along with my children in our ancestral village for a long time. Such was the state of fear. Women and trees became barren. If the Army could go back to the barracks, the corpses would come alive, walking again. Every thing, every incident would travel backwards, and Time would move again. This time around you would make sure the same was not repeated, unlike before. Then you would write a new history.

Our cries and our pains would be erased. The broken string would be welded anew. Seeing my dejected face, she added:

Tor dosh naa'i (It's not your fault.)

Originally published as 'Rastay' in *Ik Aadarshwadi di Maut*, Sucheet Kitab Ghar, 2000, Lahore

How difficult it is to sneak out of a vortex, and if you do, you fall to pieces.

One must avoid getting sucked into the vortex in the first place. What one must do and what one must not! One has to find the right and truthful path. Everyone knows the straight way, but chooses to keep their eyes closed.

Don't be sad, Daisy said.

In 1969—the days of the riots—Daisy and I used to spend our time together. People used to stare at her a lot.

Our fear has turned into hatred, Daisy had said. Ayub Khan has become an icon of state tyranny for us. We have been oppressed way beyond our limit. The Bengalis have close to no representation in the Army and other high positions. Oppression gives birth to rebellion, intrigues. We are not your subjects, nor you the king. We too had fought for this country, but your people became the masters. We want to be our own master.

Let's go, I heard Daisy's voice.

When I turned to see, I encountered the same flower-like smile. Her face, framed inside her hair, shone like an early dawn surrounded by the darkness of night.

To adorn is to affirm life. She collected her long hair into a bun and added kohl to her eyes. Crimson seemed to dance on her cheeks and lips.

Every time I step out for a walk in the evening, Daisy accompanies me after adorning herself a little.

'My friend,' she pulled my hand with love.

'Let's go,' I replied.

She laughed again, like the bell-shaped white-and-purple flowers were set into a laughing fit by the breeze. Then, while she was laughing, her face suddenly began to resemble the statue in front of us. Serious, quiet, all-contemplating, all-knowing, God's eye—the inscription at the statue's feet read: 'The watching Buddha'.

The five rivers coursing through the soul and heart, and the restlessness of the ignited fire of desire. The sorrow that is born out of them, the border and beyond. Daisy gazed at the statue. Gently, she let go of my hand and we renewed walking.

On both sides the trees had dropped flowers in piles as though to welcome us. At times like this I don't need anyone except Daisy. Only she knows the essence of a walk. I have left everyone else behind to seek her closeness. Or else these trees, this land knows my soul. They are all aware this walk has become my need. I feel its pangs inside. Its desire rises like a rebellion in me. Like ecstasy it flows in my veins. Every element of my being longs for it. I crave it the way I feel hungry for bread and thirsty for water.

I walk calmly, one step after another, neither slow, nor hasty. When my inner colours change, this is the time when I feel it— the time of evening, of leaves falling, of weather changing, sprouting of new seeds, blossoming of flowers, arrival of summer, knock of winter; everything arises to present itself before me. Even things I am used to seeing one way now appear before me with a new hat.

The rhythm my heart creates; the clamour of blood coursing through my veins. As the birds twitter, the conversations of trees are whispered into my ear—I know this is the moment when earth offers its amore to me. It is through the journey I make that I offer my eyes in her honour. In response, she opens up her breast to me. Her body resembles my body, her veins mine, her breath moves as though inside my breast, her heartbeat in my heart, her restlessness like mine; and she's a drifter like my wandering feet. I look at her astounded.

During this walk, I have chiselled my own beloved. Quietly and reluctantly! Looking at her, from near, from far. I keep chiselling it and falling in love. I carve its hands and feet; then I sculpt its eyes; then I put kohl in its eyes; place a rose in its hand, adorn it. Is it my beloved, or myself? No, no, this is not mine. I demolish it in order to sculpt it anew. This time I offer it more of myself, adding plenty and pretty colours; yet in the end it resembles me again, refuses to step outside of me. Each time new and each time my spitting image. Or is it perhaps that I am

Azra   Waqar

born anew each time? When I carve my beloved, it talks to me. If I apply one colour on it, it hands me the next one.

I stole a sideways glance at Daisy, and she blushed to death laughing.

Daisy, oh Daisy. Nervous, I reached for her hand.

Where were you?

Me? Here, right next to you.

But you live where the Karnafali flows, where it descends into the ocean, where fishermen cast their nets to catch fish; Chittagong, Rangamati, Sundarban, tea gardens, where the floods come and where the fishermen's village after village wash away, where cyclones visit and the huts fly off as though they had never existed.

Why are your eyes moist?

There is this wave rising and crashing into the ocean of life. It throws me down sometimes; sometimes offers me its arms. Sometimes laughter, sometimes tears, love and hate, happiness and sorrow, lies and truths, all so jumbled up.

Just like in a game—every sentiment is exaggerated. The waves arrive, in good humour, to the shore, depositing all the treasures they possess, and then gobble up whatever falls in their retreating path. What comes in—a treasure or separation from the beloved. No one knows.

Do you remember you and I used to climb the hills near your house in Chittagong? How easy to forget that these are the Margala hills! People jog past me. People with important names. But I search for you. That's why I end up reaching you as I journey through anything.

I used to sweat so profusely when we climbed hills, but you would be laughing. Once we had a bet: whoever gets there and touches the piece of cloth hanging by the tree wins. But as we got there, we found a dervish sitting there in a colourful garb. That is how things appear. They change appearances once you approach them. As you climb, there is only one path to the peak before you, but on the other side as you descend you come to recognize the entire length of it, back and forth. We used to go up and down every day. The colour of the hill seemed light when we climbed, but dark while coming down. We used to talk about it every time. Here too, once, as I was climbing the Margala hills, I thought there were things beyond human grasp. The sunrays fell on the dark sides of the hill in the evening. When I looked inside, I witnessed absolute darkness. It is evening. Let's go back, you had said.

Time plays games with humans. While it keeps moving forward itself, it freezes the one who stays behind, loses tracks, in stories to be penned. It is too powerful. It knocks down every invincible figure. It makes humans laugh sometimes, and makes them weep too; and yet keeps moving forward with a straight, expressionless face; never looks back, I reflected as I retraced my steps.

The history has been written down. Time has played its trick. We've been separated.

Daisy, o' Daisy, don't let go off my hand, I had said.

I never get tired of Daisy's company. She has helped me travel from confinement to freedom, has made me see beauty from ugliness, and after recognizing beauty how to lay my claim on it. She has guided me to be able to separate a knotted mess, showed me how to see 'no' from 'yes'. She is the most beautiful woman, the beauty of Bengal. When Bengal separated from us, I stole her into my heart and came back. She has been with me ever since. She is love, strength; she is the path, the way to sculpt, to create, the magic of Bengal. Long, dark hair, wheat-complexion, ocean-eyed, sweet laughter hiding in her eyelashes. She is the one who loves with her soul, the one who gives you courage. She resides in my heart like a memory that can never be erased.

—*Translated from the Punjabi by Moazzam Sheikh*

Azra Waqar

notes on contributors

Talat Abbasi was born in Lucknow, grew up in Karachi, was educated at St Joseph's College there, Kinnaird College, Lahore, and the London School of Economics. She has been living in New York since 1978 has worked for the UN. She has widely published her stories in various literary magazines, and her stories have been broadcast on the BBC. Her collection *Bitter Gourd and Other Stories* was recently published by Oxford University Press, Karachi.

Gulalai Ahad lives in Sacramento. She translates Pashtu fiction into English, and English into Pashtu, in her spare time. She is an engineer by profession.

Zubair Ahmed teaches English literature at Islamia College, Lahore. He has a collection of Punjabi poetry to his name also. His story *The Door is Open* is taken from his maiden collection *Meenh, Bohey te Baariyan*.

Amna Ali was born in Lahore. She received her higher education at Rutgers and Cornell University. She is an avid student of classical Punjabi literature.

Nadir Ali began his artistic career in the mid 1970s by writing Punjabi poetry. Two collections of his short stories have been published so far. His *Feeqa's Death* is taken from *Kahani Lekha*. After having lived in the US for ten years, he moved back with his family to Lahore where he is currently working on putting together three more collections of his short stories.

Elizabeth Bell is a San-Francisco based translator of French and Spanish who also collaborates with Moazzam Sheikh.

Asif Farrukhi was born in 1959 in Karachi. After finishing MBBS, he received his master's from Harvard University in Public Health. He is a short story writer, translator, and critic. He is also the chief editor of *Duniyazad*, a noted Urdu literary review from Karachi, where he makes his home. He is currently affiliated with the World Health Organization.

Asadullah Ghazanfar was born in Afghanistan and spent his formative years in Pakistan due to the ongoing war in his native country. He went to Peshawar University. He is regarded as one of the foremost writers in the Pashtu language.

Syed Afzal Haider was born in Jhansi. He migrated to Pakistan in August 1947. After moving to the US as a young man, he started writing in the 1980s, and is now co-editor of the *Chicago Quarterly Review*. His work was included in the *Dragonfly in the Sun: 50 years of Pakistani Writing in English*.

Intizar Husain is Pakistan's foremost Urdu writer. He was born in Dibai (India) in 1925. He moved to Lahore after Partition. He has several novels, collections of short stories and essays, and translations to his credit. He has received numerous literary awards in Pakistan, India, Europe and the US.

Ikramullah is among the major writers of Urdu from Pakistan. His novel *Gurg-e Shab* was banned by General Zia-ul-Haq. He has been widely translated into English. The story in this anthology was taken from his collection *Jungle.* He makes his home in Lahore.

Aquila Ismail was raised in East Pakistan, now Bangladesh. Later she taught at NED, Karachi. Currently she makes her home in the UAE. She writes freelance articles on women's issues for *Dawn.* Among others, she has translated the Urdu novel, *Zinda Bahar Lane* by Fahmida Riaz into English (City Press, 2000).

Soniah Naheed Kamal was born in Karachi, Pakistan and brought up in England and Saudi Arabia. She currently lives in the US. She graduated from St John's College with a BA honours in History of Mathematics and Sciences, Comparative Literature and Music. Her graduate thesis, 'On Prince Charmings, Frogs, Love Marriages and Arranged Ones', won the St John's 1996 Susan Irene Roberts prize. Her short stories have been published in Pakistan and the US. She has also adapted Oscar Wilde's play *An Ideal Husband* for an eastern audience. She writes a weekly social satire column for the Sunday *Daily Times* in Pakistan. She is also working on her novel *An Isolated Incident*.

Sorayya Khan got her early education in Europe and the International School, Islamabad, and higher education in the US. In Canada, her story *In the Shadow of the Margalla Hills* won the Malahat Review's 1995 First Novella Prize. She was a Fulbright research scholar in 1999-2000 in Pakistan and Bangladesh to research her novel *Noor* published in 2003.

Asad Mohammad Khan was born in Bhopal in 1932. He was a student at the J. J. College of Art, Bombay, Jinnah College, Karachi, Sindh Muslim Art College, Karachi, and Karachi University. He has tried his luck as a commercial artist, publisher, clerk, assistant station master, travel agent, English teacher, radio newsreader. He started his literary career as a poet, later switching to writing short stories. This story has been taken from his collection *Burj-e Khamoshan*. He lives with his wife and children in Karachi.

Ashu Lal is a doctor by profession. He is known for his poetry in Siraiki. He is new to the field of Siraiki fiction.

Muhammad Umar Memon is one of the most highly regarded translators of Urdu fiction into English. He himself is a writer of Urdu prose. He is a professor of Urdu, Persian, and Islamic Studies at the University of Wisconsin, Madison. He is chief editor of *The Annual of Urdu Studies*.

Faiza Rana is a promising young Punjabi writer who is married to a veteran Punjabi fiction writer, Maqsood Saqib. The husband-and-wife team publishes *Pancham*, a highly respected Punjabi literary review, and runs a Punjabi bookstore and a publishing house as well. They both live in Lahore.

Fahmida Riaz is a renowned Urdu poet, fiction writer and an activist. In 1977, she received the Hemmet Hellman Award by Human Rights Watch. Her *Badan Dareeda* is considered a landmark in feminist Urdu poetry. She is also the author of a highly acclaimed novella, *Godavari*. Under Zia's martial law, she lived in exile in India. Her latest collection of Urdu short stories is *Khat-e-Marmuz*.

Javed Shaheen is a renowned Urdu poet. His novel *Ik Dewar ki Duri* received critical acclaim. A collection of his novella and short stories is forthcoming. He lives in Lahore.

Zahur-ul-Haq Sheikh was born in Sialkot. He earned his master's in English literature from Government College, Lahore, worked as a lecturer at Shah Husain College, Lahore, and later served in the Civil Service in the Planning and Development Board, Punjab. This story is taken from his collection of short stories, *Talkhaabian*, published in 1992.

Vali Ram Vallabh was born in the small town of Mitthi in the region of Tharparkar, Sindh. He graduated from Sindh University. He is most renowned for his translations into Sindhi. He writes both poetry and prose.

Azra Waqar lives in Islamabad with her husband and children. Her story 'Paths' is taken from her collection *Ik Aadarshwadi di Maut*.

copyright acknowledgements

Grateful acknowledgement is made to the following for permission to reprint copyright material:

Ibn-e Hasan Press for 'The Squatter' by Asad Mohammad Khan, originally published as 'Ghus Betthiya' in the author's collection *Burj-e-Khamoshan*;

Talus Review, Spring 2002 for 'Papa's Girl' by Soniah Naheed Kamal;

Rut Lekha Publications for 'The Door Is Open' by Zubair Ahmed, originally published as 'Buha Khulla Aye' in the author's collection *Meenh, Boohe te Baarian*;

Savera, Fall 2000 and *Annual of Urdu Studies,* No. 15 for 'If Truth Be Told' by Javed Shaheen, originally published as 'Aik Haqeeqat Ka Aetraaf';

Scheherzad Publishers for 'Barriers That Remained' by Vali Ram Vallabh, originally published as 'Haden Jo Phlaangi Na Ja Sakeen' in the author's collection *Zindagi Se Ka Ta Hua Tukra*;

Sang-e Meel Publishers for 'Jungle' by Ikramullah, originally published in the author's collection *Jungle*;

Rut Lekha Publishers for 'Feeqa's Death' by Nadir Ali, originally published as 'Feeqe di Moat' in the author's collection *Kahani Lekha*;

Sang-e Meel Publishers for 'A Letter from India' by Intizar Husain, originally published as 'Hindustan Se Ek Khat' in the author's collection *Kacchve*;

Savera, No. 42 1990 for 'Spots' by Zahur-ul-Haq Sheikh, originally published as 'Dhabbey';

Pancham, June-July 2002 for 'Mangoes in the Time of Winter' by Ashu Lal, originally published as 'Poh Manh De Amb';

Pancham, June-July 2002 for 'The Tie That Binds' by Faiza Rana, originally published as 'Saanjh';

Maktaba-e Danyal for 'The Homebound' by Asif Farrukhi, originally published as 'Ghar Ghusna' in the author's collection *Shehr-e Majira*;

Dastanoon, Winter 2002 for 'Old Men' by Asadullah Ghazanfar, originally published as 'Buzurg Tana';

Aaj, Summer/Fall 1998 for 'Hieroglyphics' by Fahmida Riaz, originally published as 'Khat-e Marmooz';

Sucheet Kitaab Ghar for 'Paths' by Azra Waqar, originally published as 'Rastay' in the author's collection *Ik Aadarshwadi di Maut.*